THE CLASSROOM

Trick Out My School!

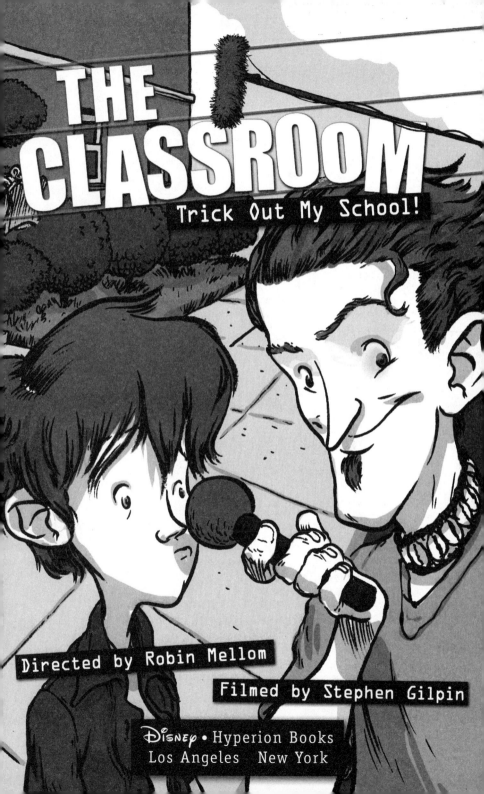

Printed in the United States
First Edition
1 3 5 7 9 10 8 6 4 2

G475-5664-5-14091

Library of Congress Cataloging-in-Publication Data

Mellom, Robin.
    The classroom : trick out my school! / directed by Robin Mellom ; filmed by Stephen
Gilpin.—First edition.
        pages cm
    Summary: When a second documentary crew arrives at Westside Middle School to film
a renowned Hollywood designer's renovations, seventh-grader Trevor Jones is chosen to
join the design team and faces a makeover of his own.
    ISBN 978-1-4231-5065-7
    [1. Middle schools—Fiction. 2. Schools—Fiction. 3. Interior decoration—Fiction.
4. Popularity—Fiction. 5. Best friends—Fiction. 6. Friendship—Fiction.
7. Documentary films—Production and direction—Fiction.]
    I. Gilpin, Stephen, illustrator. II. Title. III. Title: Trick out my school!
    PZ7.M16254Clu 2014
    [Fic]—dc23   2013029133

Reinforced binding

Visit www.DisneyBooks.com

For Jayson & Luke.
Thanks for filling our home with laughter.
—R.M.

For my mom and dad.
I'm sorry for those teenage years.
I figured you guys needed a
public acknowledgment.
—S.G.

>>Production: THE CLASSROOM

Over on Miller Street, behind the brick walls of Westside Middle School, there are desks. There are lockers. There are worksheets, textbooks, pencils, pens, and squeaky hallway floors that are buffed clean every Friday, right around four or so.

But they weren't cleaned this past Friday, since Wilson, the janitor who shall not be called the janitor, ran out of replacement filters for his floor buffer. Just thought you should know.

Now—at Westside Middle School there is a vice principal, counselors, lots of teachers, and, of course, students.

One of those students is Trevor Jones, your average, normal seventh grade student who ended up on a reality TV show.

Sort of.

This documentary crew set out to show what happens when a renowned Hollywood designer comes to trick out Westside Middle School.

And also what happens when two film crews cross paths at the same place and same time. So weird.

Westside is their middle school.

These are their stories.

Trevor Jones

7th grader
Outside homeroom,
a little perplexed

8:25 a.m.

No, I wouldn't say seventh grade has been FUN so far. That's a stretch. I would say this year has been . . . EVENTFUL. And weird. And cool. And bizarre. And epic. This year has been a lot of adjectives.

Ever since Libby was elected class president last fall, I've been busy helping her with all her presidential projects. And there have been many.

But let me be clear: when I say PROJECTS, I really mean DANCES. The girl is obsessed. She's managed to convince Vice Principal Decker to let us have a dance for virtually every occasion.

We had a Halloween dance. A Thanksgiving dance. A Leftovers from Thanksgiving dance. A Let's Hope for a Snow Day dance. (That one took place right after the Weather Seems Sorta Crummy dance.)

Libby was able to get approval for all these dances by including a fund-raiser. Decker, apparently, will agree to anything as long as you raise money for school equipment.

3

We've held bake sales, sold some of our school art projects, and even raised money by making puppets from old socks. Stuff a sock, call it a monkey, and bam! You've got yourself a moneymaker.

Our new dodgeballs are AMAZING. But Wilson keeps asking when he's going to get replacement filters for his floor buffer.

I told him I'd ask Libby if we could have a Spring Pollen dance to raise money for his filters. So I asked her . . . this morning.

Libby told me she's done with dances for now.

And that's when I saw it: a twinkle in her eye. I know what a twinkle like that means. A new presidential project. I always tell her to "think big." So I'm guessing she's come up with something HUGE.

But if it's not a dance, then what is it?

Libby Gardner

7th grader
Strangely excited,
even this early in
the morning

8:26 a.m.

No, no. I'm keeping this project a secret. At least until later this morning when Vice Principal Decker makes the announcement.

Yep, we're having an all-school assembly just to announce this project. And it's not even a fund-raiser. I've moved on to The Big Time. Soon, all of America will know about Westside Middle School.

Decker and I have been working on this for WEEKS. Planning meetings. Getting administrative approval. Signing contracts. It's been endless. So I can't believe this day is FINALLY here!

[bounces on toes]

Don't ask me how I've managed to keep all this a secret from Trevor. But he is going to love this project . . . I just know it!

Molly Decker

7th grader
Bored, as usual

8:27 a.m.

Yeah, I already know about the secret project. Since Decker is my dad, it wasn't hard to accidentally eavesdrop.

But I'm going to have to talk Dad out of this one. It is . . . oh, what's the word?

RIDICULOUS.

Wait till Trevor hears about this. He's going to FREAK.

But if anything, it's going to get interesting around here again. Because that Leftovers from Thanksgiving dance? Total snore.

CHAPTEЯ ONE

LIBBY GARDNER ENTERED MR. EVERETT'S HOMEROOM class with a clipboard in one hand and a stress ball in the other. Even though she was excited about the announcement Vice Principal Decker was about to make, she was also stressed. Would everyone be ecstatic? Would they think she was cool for putting this together? Or was this about to demolish her respectable level of popularity?

Keeping a secret this big required lots of stress relief. Unfortunately, the ball was not enough. Libby had moved on to chewing her pencil eraser. Helpful, but also a tad gross.

All the students were seated and ready to start class. Cindy Applegate, the official school gossip, was to her left, scrunching her hair to make it curlier. Libby's best friend, Trevor, was seated in the back row, doodling in his notebook. Molly had her head buried in her hands. And Mr. Everett—who was decorating his bulletin board—was currently tangled up in crepe paper.

A normal Monday. Everything's ready. It's time...

Libby glanced up at the intercom.

Click.

Here we go.

"Good morning, Westside. This is Vice Principal Decker. I have a very important announcement to make."

Libby turned around and caught Trevor's eye. She gave him a thumbs-up, and he returned with a thumbs-up.

But Trevor had no idea what he was thumbing up. Surely this was just another car wash or barbecue. Why was Libby so amped?

"Students, your seventh grade class president, Libby Gardner, has entered our school into a contest. She wrote a fabulous essay, and now"—Decker took a deep breath—"renowned designer Kip Lee will be giving our school a makeover. We are going to be on his hit TV show, *Trick Out My School!*"

The class erupted in squeals and claps. Libby could even hear the cheering from other classes down the hall. *They love it! They're excited! Popularity maintained—maybe even increased!*

It was understandable that the students would be excited, since *Trick Out My School* was the highest-rated school makeover reality show on TV. *Everyone* knew about it, mostly for its signature wild changes.

Fish tanks in the locker room.

See-through walls in the teachers' lounge.

Recliner chairs in Language Arts class.

The show always did something different, and it was always over the top.

Typically the producers of the show selected which schools would get a makeover based on the criteria of a) really needing a makeover and b) being located very close to their Burbank studio. (L.A. traffic is miserable, especially when dealing with a looming TV deadline.)

But once a year they would hold a contest and allow students from all over the state to write essays in order to win a makeover for their school. Kip and his team would then load up their trailers and travel to the winning school to renovate and shoot the show in two weeks.

It was not known yet what Kip and his crew had in store for Westside, but all would be revealed at the assembly.

Though there were many cheers and squeals, they were not coming from two people in particular: Molly and Trevor.

Molly did not like the idea of a Hollywood hotshot doing a makeover for free. No one does good work for *free*. In her words: RIDICULOUS.

Trevor also wasn't excited about this news. He didn't have a problem with Hollywood hotshots. Or people doing things for free. Or even things that were ridiculous.

Trevor had a problem with change. *Any* kind of change.

"Kip Lee is on his way from Hollywood," Decker continued. "The crew is already here and will begin doing prep work. Please look as if you're enjoying the hammering and drilling—they will be filming our reactions, and I want you all looking happy. When Kip arrives, I will call an all-school assembly. Until then, have a great day, Westside!"

Cindy Applegate turned to Libby. "Pretty cool move, Lib."

Libby twirled her hair around her finger. "Really? You think?" She was very interested in hearing Cindy say she liked her idea. After their grueling campaign race earlier in the year, nothing was more satisfying.

"It's a good idea," Cindy said as she smacked her gum. "I just hope Kip fixes the school's lighting. It's terrible for reapplying lip gloss. Think you could mention that to him?"

"Sure." Libby then pressed her lips together and stared straight ahead. The thought of meeting Kip Lee later today was causing her insides to twist.

Kip Lee was her idol. Well, *one* of them.

Libby decided to note this momentous day in her calendar.

FOUND IN LIBBY'S CALENDAR

Libby Gardner

Outside homeroom,
super chatty

8:50 a.m.

Can you believe it? I won our school a makeover!
We're going to be on TV!

See, at first I was just going to hold a car
wash fund-raiser, but it was Trevor who convinced
me to think BIG. When I saw a commercial on TV for
a contest to be on the show *Trick Out My School*,
I knew I had to go for it!

All I had to do was write a ten-thousand-word
essay and send in photographic evidence of how
dilapidated our school is. One of the pictures
I sent was of the cafeteria. Also, the inside of
Trevor's locker. Also, everything else.

So I put together the whole thing in a Power-
Point 3-D slide show, and we won! That means new
chairs, good lighting, and a much better color
scheme. No more walls the color of turkey gravy!
And I've watched EVERY episode of *Trick Out My
School*. It's possible we'll also get a shark tank.

Or neon lights in the cafeteria. Or maybe even hammocks in place of desks!

But the best part? It's Kip Lee. KIP. LEE. He's simply awesome. And as everyone knows . . . he's my IDOL. Well, actually, Barbara Boxer, senator from California, is my top idol, but he's totally in second place!

[shakes with excitement]

Oh my gosh, look at me! I'm shaking! Or maybe I forgot to eat breakfast? I'm not sure! But I DO know that I can't wait to meet Mr. Lee.

And this HAS to be exciting for Trevor, too, since he was the one who inspired me to enter the contest. He must be ECSTATIC!!

Trevor Jones

In the hallway,
super stunned

8:51 a.m.

Obviously telling Libby to "think big" was a mistake. I just meant stuff like better art supplies. Or maybe even electric pencil sharpeners. Those are awesome.

But no, apparently when you tell Libby Gardner to "think big," you end up with a big, loud, pounding monster truck of an idea.

[rubs temples]

This is all too much. I should have taken some vitamins this morning.

Marty Nelson

8th grader
By the water
fountain, super
confused

8:52 a.m.

I don't get it. A makeover? What is a MAKEOVER?!

Naw, I've never heard of the show. If it isn't on the Discovery Channel or Animal Planet, I've never seen it.

I'd be much more excited if we were getting visited by that reality show *Duck Quackers*. Making our own duck call would make way more sense than getting a disco ball in the cafeteria or whatever.

But then again . . . the floors in the boys' locker room could use some attention.

I might give the guy a chance. MIGHT.

CHAPTER TWO

TREVOR JONES TOOK TWO VITAMINS AND WISHED NIGHT-fall would come early. But it was only 10:27 in the morning, and the hammering and drilling had just begun. The prep crew was demolishing cabinets, pulling up floors, and ripping out light fixtures. Oh, the headache.

There was no way he could act as if he were happy about this makeover, not with his head pounding like this. So before third period, Trevor found himself seated on a green mesh cot in the nurse's office.

It was a cot he knew well.

The first week of school he was in there because of a love punch to the stomach from Nancy Polanski. Then there was the bump on the head from a dodgeball incident. And, of course, the never-to-be-forgotten Cafeteria

Incident, which involved an unfortunate tangled hairnet. (Long story.) But today it was just a straightforward headache caused by irritating hammering and drilling noises.

As always, Nurse Quincy was wearing her comfortable white sneakers and her hair in a tight ponytail. When Trevor entered her small office, she responded swiftly, with the same first-aid technique she used for virtually every ailment.

"Lie down and put this cold washcloth on your forehead." She kindly pointed toward the rickety green mesh cot.

Trevor was convinced you could go into the nurse's office with practically any problem, and Nurse Quincy would always offer her exact same go-to remedy.

But as strange as it was, Trevor had to admit . . . the cold-washcloth-on-the-forehead technique? *Totally* worked. Every. Single. Time.

For all he knew, public schools were the only places on earth you could find such magic washcloths.

"Just relax," Nurse Quincy said in a singsongy voice. "Your headache will be gone soon." She stood at the counter and straightened her jars of tongue depressors. She never *used* the tongue depressors; she just arranged them nicely like they were decorations. "So I guess the banging is too

17

tricked out for you, too?" she asked with a smirk.

"*Way* too much for me." Then Trevor realized she had said "you, *too*." Confused, he lifted his head, letting the washcloth fall to his side. "Do you mean I'm not the only one?"

Nurse Quincy took a few steps across the room, and

with a quick sweeping motion, she pulled back a curtain to reveal another student lying on a cot with a wet cloth covering her forehead. Trevor instantly recognized her.

Ripped rainbow tights. Clunky boots. A torn jean jacket held together with safety pins.

Molly Decker.

What was Molly doing in here? She was the most tough-minded girl he knew. But apparently even a tough-minded girl could be brought down by school renovations.

Trevor walked over and sat down on the edge of the cot, right next to her. "Molly, are you okay?"

She kept her eyes covered with the cloth as she spoke in a weak voice. "What's happening? Did I die?" She blindly waved her arms around like she was lost.

"Nope. You're in the nurse's office. At school. They have tongue depressors."

Nurse Quincy handed Trevor a couple, and he stuck one in each of Molly's hands to reassure her. She squeezed them tightly, and within moments she calmed down. Nurse Quincy folded her arms, looking content that she'd actually found a use for her tongue depressors other than decoration.

Molly used her pinkie finger to lift the washcloth above one eye to look at Trevor. "How did I get here?"

"The renovations, remember? They started hammering on the—"

"Do *not* use the word *hammer*, or I swear, Trevor, I will take this tongue depressor and—"

"Okay! No hamme—I mean . . . how do you feel now? Is the washcloth working yet?" He figured it should be working for her because his head was already feeling better.

Molly sat up and took the washcloth off. "You know what? It *is* better. Except that annoying makeover crew is still here. I kinda wish my headache would come back."

Smiling as if she knew it would all work out perfectly, Nurse Quincy tapped her watch. "You two need to hurry on to class now. The bell's about to ring for third period."

They handed back their washcloths and headed out the door. As they exited, they passed by Wilson, senior head of custodial support. He'd been promoted to senior status due to his hard work on finding and eradicating the horrible stench that had overtaken the school last fall. Not even the scientists from the Center for Disease Prevention could locate the smell—which was actually just a rotten tuna sandwich stuck in Trevor's locker. But Wilson had been the successful one, and Vice Principal Decker asked Molly to personally hand-sew a new badge for his uniform.

Molly had never sewn anything before; she just put

things together with safety pins. But Vice Principal Decker was trying to get Molly more involved in school, and he figured this would be a start. Molly had several life mottoes, and one of them was: *Just keep to yourself; people are weird.* But her dad wanted her to be more "friend-like." And every once in a while she'd give it a shot.

She'd tried very hard on Wilson's badge. She really did.

"Uh, nice badge, Wilson," Trevor said as Wilson blew past.

But Wilson kept focused on the prize ahead: that magic washcloth. He, too, suffered from tricked-out-itis. "Sorry, Trevor. Can't talk now."

They headed down the hall, which was chaotic and busy with students going to third period. Molly turned to Trevor and said, "Did you really like Wilson's badge? It wasn't as easy as it looks."

Molly was the one who'd made it? Trevor swallowed. He wasn't sure what to say. "It . . . um . . . looks like you tried hard."

"Thanks. I could sew something for you. Or try to." Molly was proud of herself for showing such friendly behavior, especially this early in the morning. When it came to Trevor, though, being friendly seemed to come easily. For everyone else? Not so much.

"Uh . . ." Trevor looked up and was relieved to see Libby standing outside class, motioning for them to come over.

A change of topic—just what I need right about now, Trevor thought.

In one hand, Libby clutched a clipboard, and in the other she was vigorously squeezing her stress ball. She rushed up to them, looking panicked.

Very panicked.

Wilson

Totally unimpressed

10:35 a.m.

I have this problem with getting headaches when I'M not the one doing the hammering or drilling.

I also have this problem with other people coming into the school and taking over.

I have OTHER problems, but that's not important right now. What IS important is keeping this school exactly the way it is. Westside has managed just fine for years. I don't understand why anyone would want to trick out a school. And I don't understand what "trick out" even means.

Plus—and no offense or anything—having ONE documentary crew here has been enough. Now we're going to have TWO crews?! What a mess. I'd better find a way to get replacement filters for my floor buffer.

[leans in, lifts a brow]

And if they touch my Supply Containment Unit . . . THEY are going to be the ones with a problem.

23

Cindy Applegate

7th grader
Bouncing on her toes

10:36 a.m.

Sure, I'm excited about Kip Lee coming to our school. I follow him on Twitter, and yesterday he put up a picture of his puppy. And also one of his half-eaten veggie burritos. So cute!!!

Being "accessible to your fans" I think is what you call it.

Anyway, I can't wait to meet him and tell him how skilled I am at using ribbon and glitter. This could be it, you know . . . the day I get DISCOVERED.

Toodles!

[skips off, unaware of the pink ribbon stuck to the bottom of her shoe]

CHAPTER THREE

"HAVE YOU SEEN HIM YET? HE'S HERE!**"**

Molly wrinkled her forehead and crossed her arms—her getting-annoyed stance. "There are lots of 'hims' here. Who are you talking about?"

"KIP. KIP LEE!" Libby said, as if this should be obvious. "He drove up in a black SUV, pulling a fancy trailer. Some people brought him a latte, some freshly squeezed juice, and he was even fitted for a new pair of sandals . . . Italian leather, I believe. I'm not sure—my binoculars started to fog up. Kip should be in here any minute. Have you seen him?" She squeezed her stress ball, popped up on her toes, and scanned the busy hallway.

Trevor crossed his arms, annoyed. She'd never even told him about the contest, though she knew ALL TOO WELL that he was allergic to change. And now all she could talk about was Kip this, Kip that. He hadn't even met the guy and he was already tired of him. "Who cares if Kip is here yet? Does it matter?" Trevor asked.

Libby gasped—dramatically—then took three hard steps closer to him so that they were practically nose to nose. Actually, forehead to nose, since Libby was a tad taller. "Does. It. *Matter?*" She flipped her clipboard around to show a list of all the facts she had gathered on Kip and his TV show—where it was filmed, how many viewers, number of sponsors, and so on. It was totally thorough. This was Libby Gardner, after all.

Attached to the top of Libby's clipboard was a picture of Kip Lee. Some would describe him as "rather dashing." Or: "handsome." Also: "Hottie McHotster."

When Molly got a glimpse of him, all she could do was roll her eyes. Intrigued, Trevor also took a quick peek. He wondered how the guy could get his hair to look *that* perfect while simultaneously looking *that* messy. Probably very expensive gel and way too much time available in the morning.

Molly elbowed Libby to get her attention. "It's a TV show. He's some Hollywood hotshot. He'll only come out of his trailer when there's a camera around."

Libby blinked a couple of times, taking this in. "Huh. You're probably right. See you guys at the assembly." Then she slowly turned, no longer squeezing the life out of the stress ball, and calmly strolled on to her next class.

"Wow. You calmed her down in a hurry."

Molly shrugged. "There's really nothing to get excited about."

Trevor tilted his head. "You are very hard to figure out, Molly Decker."

"And why's that?"

"Isn't having our school on a reality show at least *interesting*? You're the one who always says it's too boring around here."

FOUND ON LIBBY'S CLIPBOARD

Molly planted her hands on her hips and looked at him like what she was about to say was as easy as changing the color of your hair highlights. "Listen carefully. It's simple. There are *two* kinds of interesting. There's *actual* interesting, and then there's *annoying* interesting."

"Mmm-hmm," Trevor said in an agreeable tone as if he were agreeing, but really he was baffled—he was already twelve years old, and he had no idea there were two different kinds of interesting. Wow.

"So *actual* interesting," Molly continued, "is when things happen like you run for class president but try to throw the race."

Trevor nodded. "Yep, I guess that was actually interesting." Though he also cringed at the memory of him throwing the seventh-grade-class-president election. Oh, the drama.

"Okay, so things that are *annoying* interesting?" Molly counted them on her fingers. "The smell of gasoline. Car alarms. That trail that snails leave behind." When they reached the door of Ms. Ferrell's math class, she stopped and turned to him. "And also? It's annoying interesting when some Hollywood dude comes to 'trick out' your school and all the hammering and drilling gives you a headache." She looked around and lowered her voice, to make sure no one else could hear. "And if they dare mess with my Thinking Stall, they're going to pay."

Trevor scratched his head. "You have a Thinking Stall?"

"Girls' bathroom, fourth stall down. That's where I get my best thinking done. And my best drawings, too. I say save the Thinking Stalls. And everything else," Molly said. "We don't need change."

HAMMERS ARE ALWAYS UP TO NO GOOD.

FOUND ON BATHROOM WALL

Trevor was starting to see her side of things. "I'm not a huge fan of change."

And he wasn't. Not at all. In fact, over the years, he'd hardly changed anything about his bedroom: not the rug, not the paint color, not even the arrangement of the furniture.

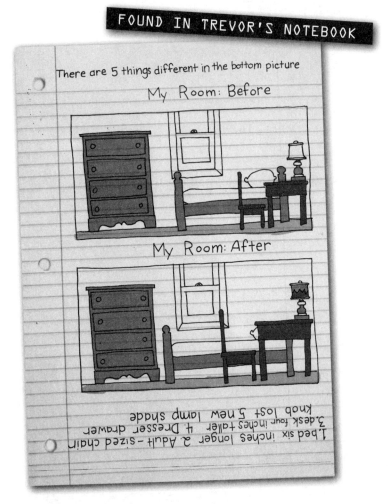

FOUND IN TREVOR'S NOTEBOOK

There are 5 things different in the bottom picture

My Room: Before

My Room: After

1. bed six inches longer 2. Adult-sized chair
3. desk four inches taller 4. Dresser drawer
knob lost 5. new lamp shade

The only change he did agree to? When his mom tried to get him to give away his old toys, he agreed to put them away in his closet, out of sight. He simply wanted them available in case they had a visitor—perhaps someone with a small son who needed toys for him to play with. It could happen. No sense in being unprepared.

So far, Trevor's "no big changes" life rule had worked out quite well, so he really didn't see why they needed to suddenly make all these big changes at school.

He leaned in closer and whispered, "To be honest, I don't like change at all. In fact, I still have my stuffed animals."

Molly held a hand up. "Whoa. No need to overshare."

He swallowed hard, realizing he needed to change the subject before he started talking about all the LEGO boxes he kept in his closet, too. (For emergencies!)

A crowd of people pushed past them, and one of them called out, "See you at lunch, Trevor!"

Looking up, he realized it was Mr. Jeffries, the art teacher. Perfect timing, Trevor thought. A distraction from my continuing all this oversharing.

Trevor waved at him. "Yep. See you at lunch, Mr. J!"

"What was that about?" Molly asked.

"I've been helping him organize the art supplies a few days a week during lunch, and in return he's been giving me drawing lessons. He's awesome. You should come with me! Then we won't hear all the hammering and drilling."

The art room at Westside was the perfect place to escape, since it also doubled as the band room, which meant it was lined with soundproof walls that would drown out all the hammering sounds. (But, in the interest of full disclosure, the art room tripled as a meeting spot for the PTA, so it was often littered with muffin wrappers.)

"Come on, Molly. We could hang out at lunch and draw. It may even be better than stall number four."

Molly tugged on the ends of her hair while she thought this over. "But isn't Libby going to be mad that we aren't happy about the makeover?"

"We don't have to *tell* her we aren't excited—it'll hurt her feelings. We'll just hide out in the art room and stay away. Besides, once she meets Kip Lee she'll be so distracted, she won't even think about us."

Molly nodded. "A pretty good plan. And hey—I know I say I don't get excited very often. And do not repeat this out loud or I'll deny it and probably strangle you, but . . . I am excited about taking drawing lessons."

"Molly!" He poked her on the arm. "You're . . . excited?"

"Settle down." Molly smiled—it was slight but it was there.

Trevor liked it when Molly Decker smiled. It was like a shooting star; if you catch a glimpse of it, consider yourself lucky.

The bell rang, and Trevor and Molly headed into class and settled in their seats. Then once again, the intercom clicked on. "I need your attention, students. It's time for the assembly," Vice Principal Decker said with unusual pep. "There's someone very important I want you all to meet."

Libby—seated in the very front row of her class—squirmed in her chair with excitement. She knew the wait was over—this was it. She was about to meet her second-place IDOL.

Kip Lee.

Libby Gardner

Outside the gym,
pacing, rather
giddy

10:50 a.m.

Ohmygosh, ohmygosh, ohmygosh. Kip Lee . . . is . . .
HERE. Oh, wow . . .

[clutches stomach, bends over for a few seconds]

Hang on, gotta catch my breath.

Maybe you should go interview someone else
first—no. Wait! The feeling is starting to come
back in my fingers. I'm OKAY!

Anyway, I can't wait to meet him. Maybe he'll
talk to me after the assembly or something. I want
to tell him how much I admire his design work and
how much I LOVED the organizational cabinets he
installed on episode twelve of season two. They're
my DREAM cabinets. I mean, no one can design as
well as Kip . . . oh, sheesh . . .

[bends over]

Yeah, you should probably just interview someone else. I can't feel my toes now.

34

WESTSIDE
MIDDLE SCHOOL
MAKEOVER
DAY ONE

CHAPTER FOUR

THE ENTIRE SCHOOL—ALL SEVENTH AND EIGHTH GRADE classes—filed into the gym for a Sudden Assembly. Vice Principal Decker stood on the stage and directed students where to sit so he could get started quickly.

He was eager to introduce Kip Lee. This was one of the most exciting assemblies he'd ever experienced in all his years as a middle school vice principal. And he'd worked as a vice principal at *a lot* of schools. But today—TODAY— was going to be a different kind of assembly. He'd even worn his favorite bow tie for the occasion. His *only* bow tie, truthfully.

Usually his Sudden Assemblies were about new rules or strange smells or small animals on the loose. (That last one was at his previous middle school, and they finally trapped

The *Gazette*

85¢

Wiley Weasel
FINALLY CAPTURED!

Old Lady Grow
Huge Tomato
by Craig Miller

Agnes Flewharty, the ol
woman in Galesburg an
gardener, presented the
of the Four Corners Ga
ing Society's annual ve
competition with the m
midable entry in the te
category they had see
years. The "Brain Te
variety that easily to
place in the "heirloo
bracket, first place c
the entire tomato cr
and won Ms. Flewh
medal. After a gra
ceptance speech in
said, "I just stuck
the ground and wa
from time to time
brain surgery," s
she'd take good
medal and stick
bottom drawer c
bench in the ga
keeps any othe
might have w

Vice Principal Decker woos weasel from soccer goal.

Photo by:
Nathan Simpson

Vice Principal Decker of Galesburg
Middle School succeeded in not
only locating but al
a weasel that had c
school's science r
wasn't sure it th
uld be for meatloaf

thought, 'well I like meatloaf and
so does my dog', and we just gave
it a try," he related.
were minor an

NEWSPAPER ARTICLE FOUND
IN THE GAZETTE

the weasel in the soccer field goal using a piece of day-old meat loaf.)

In the front row, Libby wriggled in her metal chair, unable to contain her excitement. She couldn't believe that she was finally getting a chance to see the one and only Kip Lee. And not just that, but listen to him talk about his thoughts on design, loudly—*into a microphone*!

"Students, we have a special guest with us today— a *very* special guest." Vice Principal Decker gripped the microphone tightly. "As you know, our seventh grade class president, Libby Gardner, entered our school in a contest, and now"—he took a deep breath—"designer Kip Lee himself is here to make over Westside Middle School for his hit TV show, *Trick Out My School!*"

The students broke out in wild applause. It was the first time Vice Principal Decker had seen students *this* excited at a school assembly. He knew wearing that bow tie was a good idea.

"Kip and his crew drove here all the way from Hollywood!" The audience squirmed in their seats, looking around for Kip Lee to make his entrance. Decker straightened his bow tie and continued. "And now Mr. Kip Lee himself will say some things to the school. Come on out here!"

From the side of the stage, a rugged, slim, spray-tanned man emerged. He wore designer jeans, Italian leather sandals, a crisp white T-shirt, and several shell necklaces. Very beachy.

Kip strutted up to the microphone and looked out at the excited audience. He took a moment. Looked around. Raised an eyebrow. Then finally: "What's up, Westside?"

Pandemonium overcame the crowd. Though to be accurate, most of the screaming and general wildness came from the girls.

In the back row, Trevor and Molly looked at each other and rolled their eyes. Trevor didn't understand why all these girls were so impressed with a guy who clearly used far too much max-hold hair gel. And Molly wondered why all these people were clapping for a guy who might demolish her Thinking Stall. So lame.

Kip Lee paced back and forth across the stage, then said, "Two words: Comfortable. Seating. *That* is why I am here. You can't be expected to spend your day in old, squeaky chairs. My goal is for you to be comfortable while you sit. And then to look good while you sit. That is what a good designer does. Repeat after me: we deserve comfortable yet stylish seating!"

"We deserve comfortable yet stylish seating!" the makeover mob chanted.

Molly leaned over to Trevor and whispered, "Can you believe this? Everyone's going nuts for him. And my own father is even wearing a bow tie." She bent over and put her head between her knees. "I can't take this. It's ridiculous."

Trevor patted her on the back. "Ridiculous."

Libby, however, was bouncing with anticipation of whatever words Kip was about to say next. Her rickety old metal chair squeaked while she bounced. Kip is right, she thought. Comfortable seating is so important. She turned to the person next to her and whispered, "He is a genius."

But Libby was so caught up with everything happening

on the stage, she didn't even notice who the person was sitting next to her. It was Cindy Applegate. Even though Cindy had told her earlier that she liked this idea of a school makeover, Libby was still curious what Cindy *really* thought. Did she have other motives? Cindy was not exactly the most trustworthy seventh grader she'd ever met.

"Yep, he's brilliant," Cindy said with a smirk. "I already told him that on Twitter last night. He hasn't replied to me yet, but I'm sure he will soon."

Last night? How'd she know that Kip was coming? Libby wondered.

As if Cindy could read her mind, Cindy answered. "My mom found out about Kip coming from her cousin who heard it from her chiropractor who heard it from Kip's hairstylist."

Darn, Libby thought. Gossip flies fast. And why didn't I think of introducing myself to him on Twitter?

Kip worked the stage as he spoke, expertly tossing the microphone cord out of his path, like he'd done this many times before. Which, of course, he *had*, since the name of the show was *Trick Out My School* and holding assemblies on stages with cords while still looking ruggedly handsome and tan was all part of his job.

"You should be very proud that your school won this

year's makeover," Kip said. "We had hundreds of entries, but Westside Middle School's essay stood out above them all!"

As the audience clapped, Libby turned to Cindy and whisper-yelled, "That's us. He's talking about *our* school!"

"I'm completely aware of this." Cindy's face reddened. Deep down, she wished *she* had been the one who'd been elected student class president and had entered them in contests and was getting attention during Sudden Assemblies.

Kip stopped walking and talking to face the audience. "And now, Westside . . . you can thank your seventh grade class president for writing that winning essay . . . Libby Gardner!"

The crowd cheered and turned in their seats to get a look at her. Libby said to the side of Cindy's face, "That's me. He's saying my name."

"Yep. Got it." Cindy looked up at the ceiling and clenched her jaw.

"Libby Gardner," Kip called out, "come on up to the stage with me!"

"He used my name again," Libby said, still looking at Cindy.

"And he asked you to go up onstage."

"What?"

"You! Go up on the stage!" Cindy bumped shoulders with her. "Hurry, before *I* go up there!"

Libby shuddered. "He wants me to . . . what?" She had known she was going to meet Kip, but in all the other shows it was just a quick meeting in the hallway or by his black SUV. But now he wanted her to come meet him . . . *onstage?* This was unreal!

Libby looked around and cringed when she saw that all eyes were on her. This attention was making her nervous. Then she noticed that up on the stage, Kip Lee—*the* Kip Lee—was motioning for her to join him.

This meant she was going to meet him. Talk to him. See his beachy necklaces up close.

And this also meant she was now going to possibly throw up. Or go numb in the nose.

But she took a deep breath and pushed her nervous feelings away because—ohmygosh—this was Kip Lee . . . her second-favorite idol!

Get it together, Libby, she coached herself. *Don't go fan-girl crazy now. No one likes creepy.*

Libby hopped up out of her chair (with the help of a quick shove from Cindy) and stepped onto the stage next to the most wondrous designer. Live. In person. Approximately eight inches away. And Libby could hardly breathe.

"Libby here wrote a fantastic essay to win the contest. Probably the best one we've ever seen," Kip explained to the audience. "But there is a lot of work to be done for this remodel. So, Libby, I have a surprise for you. Since you won the contest for your school, you get to be part of our design team. We'd like you to work with the crew during lunch throughout the makeover. What do you say?"

Libby's stomach fell through the stage floor and onto the ground. Not literally. But pretty much.

"Absolutely!" she yelped, and gave a clap.

Trevor watched in shock. He wasn't shocked by the fact that Libby would willingly give up her free time during lunch. It was the clapping and the yelping. This was something he'd expect from Cindy. But Libby? It appeared this Kip Lee was bringing out a different side of his best friend, and he wasn't sure he liked it.

"Is Libby going to do a backflip or what?" Molly whispered.

Trevor shook his head and crinkled his forehead. "Honestly . . . she may. I can't watch."

"And there's more!" Kip said, raising a finger in the air, silencing the audience. "Libby also gets to ask one other person to join our team and be her design partner. So, Westside . . . who's it going to be?!"

Immediately the crowd squealed with excitement and many hands raised, but one hand in particular raised higher than all the rest. Cindy Applegate's. "Libby, please! Pick me! I know colors. I know design! I KNOW COLORS!"

Mr. Lee rubbed his forehead. "Young lady, enough with the bouncing—I'm getting dizzy here."

Cindy nodded and tried to contain her excitement, but she wasn't doing a very good job of it, because she was teetering on her toes on top of her chair.

Libby surveyed the hands raised. She felt bad she

couldn't ask all of them, so really there wasn't any choice to make—she knew *exactly* whom to pick. Libby locked eyes with Trevor and smiled.

Since this whole thing was inspired by Trevor's great advice, she absolutely *had* to choose him to help with the renovation. And giving him a chance to work alongside a famous designer and all-around fantastic guy Kip Lee? Trevor was going to freak!

Scrunching down lower in his seat, Trevor wondered why in the world Libby was looking at him like that. Oh no, he thought. Why do I get the feeling something humiliating is about to happen?

Libby pulled the microphone from Kip Lee's hand and called out, "I choose Trevor Jones!"

Molly snapped her head up and turned to Trevor. "No way," she whispered. "Don't do it. Tell her no."

"But—"

"Come on up, Tyler," Kip Lee said.

"It's Trevor," Libby corrected him.

Glancing back and forth between Molly and Libby, Trevor hesitated, trying to decide what to do. But then he noticed a new camera crew filming him. The crew from *Trick Out My School* was recording every moment of this.

So what *could* he do? Make some sort of a scene right

there in front of the entire school? In front of all of America?!

Sure, it would make things interesting for Molly, but it would make things awful for him and Libby. Except the last thing he wanted to do was give up his lunch break, since he was going to get drawing lessons from Mr. Jeffries with Molly.

Trevor didn't really see that he had much choice, though. He shrugged at Molly, then scuffled up to the front of the room and joined Libby on the stage with Kip Lee. It was bad enough for Trevor that he was now in front of the entire school in an uncomfortable situation. But then Mr. Lee waved over a man from the back of the room. "You're rolling, right?" Kip asked.

A man holding a large video camera nodded.

"We need footage for the show," Kip explained to Trevor and Libby. "I want you two to look into the camera and say 'This is *Trick Out My School*' and maybe do a thumbs-up or something super fun like that. Got it?" He then turned to the audience and said, "We need you to cheer, Westside! Your new makeover team will be led by Libby and Tucker! Let's hear it!!"

The crowd went nuts, cheering, clapping, and standing on chairs, much to Wilson's dislike.

All the wild squeals and clapping caused Trevor's stomach to twist in knots. Earlier in the year he'd been wildly popular for 1.6 weeks, and then it all ended. Abruptly. Painfully. But then he got involved in Libby's projects, so he started receiving *some* attention. Though he would consider himself only *mildly* popular. Some high fives in the hall and people lending him paper when he ran out. That's about it. It was respectable, though. All was well.

But *this*? Being the center of the entire school's frenzied attention? It was a lot of pressure. He'd been down that road before—extreme popularity meant not making any embarrassing mistakes. It was not his favorite road.

Kip motioned for the cameraman to start filming. "And three . . . two . . . one . . . wait!" Kip then reached into his toolbox, pulled out a hammer, and handed it to Trevor. "You should hold this, Travis."

Immediately, when Trevor saw the hammer, he felt a headache come on. A change-is-not-good headache. It was too much pressure—there was no way he could go through with this. He wished he'd listened to Molly.

Rubbing his right temple, Trevor looked directly into the camera and said, "I need to go see the school nurse."

Then he turned, jumped off the stage, and ran out of the room.

So much for not making a scene.

Cindy Applegate

By the gym door,
bouncing on her toes

11:20 a.m.

Did you hear what he said? Kip Lee! He called me "young lady"! Those are such nice words. Admiration, I think you call it. He probably figured out that was ME sending all those nice messages to him on Twitter last night. Twenty-seven messages, to be exact. I'm sure he'll get back to me soon.

So, anyway? It makes perfect sense that Libby didn't pick me to be on the design team. She doesn't want Kip to be totally impressed with all my design ideas and amazing work ethic and natural curls. Also, my ability to wrap gifts in under a minute. And I'm guessing he'll offer me a summer internship when he finds out I'm SUPER advanced at the skill of picking out cute ribbon and sprinkling glitter. It's something I was born with.

Now I just have to find a way to get Kip to pay attention to ME.

Not Libby.

Corey Long

8th grader

Already full of self-confidence, even before noon

11:21 a.m.

Sure, I'm only in eighth grade, but I could totally do that Kip guy's job. My mom's been sending me to acting classes because she wants me to star on a TV sitcom or have my own reality show by the time I'm sixteen. Or maybe fourteen, depending on when I make the Olympic swim team.

Anyway, my mom got all excited when she found out Kip Lee was coming here. I knew it was a surprise, or whatever, so I was cool about it. And now she wants me to talk to him for pointers and study him and stuff.

So far the dude gets props for all that fancy slinging of the microphone cord—pretty smooth.

But I TOTALLY have better hair. He probably has questions for me.

Trevor Jones

Outside the nurse's
office, pressing his
temples

11:22 a.m.

No. I am NOT excited about Kip Lee being here. I don't like hammers or the sounds associated with them. And I am not a fan of change.

Like, you know how in elementary school when the teacher would change the seating arrangement every month? Everyone would get all excited because they got to go sit in some new exotic part of the room, but for me it was like floating in the middle of the sea. I was constantly looking around trying to get my bearings—where was the board, the pencil sharpener, the clock, the nearest exit? It took me nearly a month to finally get comfortable, and then BAM! New seating arrangement. Pretty horrible.

So do I like the idea of this Kip Lee guy doing a complete school makeover of Westside? No. Not one bit. I mean, we already have ONE film crew here, and now we're going to have ANOTHER one?

That's twice as many cameras. So twice the chance of my doing something humiliating and having it end up on TV. Isn't simply surviving seventh grade ENOUGH pressure?

CHAPTER FIVE

O N THE STAGE IN FRONT OF THE ENTIRE SCHOOL, Libby stood stiff as a Popsicle stick, not knowing what to do. Murmurs and whispers filled the room as everyone wondered why Trevor had run off the stage.

"Want to pick someone else?" Kip asked Libby.

She didn't know why Trevor left. But it had to be for a good reason, and she needed to find out what it was. "Can we record the footage later?" She winced, shocked that she actually had the nerve to say this to Kip Lee. "Just let me go find Trevor. I can fix this."

He leaned in, covering the microphone so the audience couldn't hear. "If it means not picking that bouncing girl in the front row, then fine."

Libby smiled, then ran off the stage, through the audience, and out the door.

Trevor was just steps away from the nurse's office and mere moments away from the healing effects of that magic washcloth. He hoped it had the ability to fix headaches *and* personal problems.

But before he could reach the door, Libby grabbed him by the shoulder. "Are you sick? I wasn't sure what to tell Kip. Are you going to help?"

"I, um . . . you know . . . headache?" Trevor didn't want to let her down or anything, but all this change wasn't what he had in mind. Maybe just some extra paintbrushes for Mr. Jeffries's art class. But *this*—a whole school makeover, a reality show, cameras, clipboards, stress balls—it was all so . . . excessive. How could he explain that she needed to tone it down? Not exactly an easy thing to say.

But he had to start somewhere. "Here's the thing, Lib. I'm not sure we need all this change. A school makeover?"

She put her hand on her hip. "I'm aware of your no-changes-in-life policy, Trevor, but maybe it's time for you to—"

"Change things up—I know." He was getting pretty good at finishing her sentences during a lecture.

"You still have your stuffed animals."

"Available for *loan*," he clarified. "In case someone brings over a small child and they request a stuffed bear or owl or turtle or—"

"What about the furniture in your room?" She crossed her arms. "You've never even moved a single item since you were born."

"Yes, I have."

"I'm talking about *furniture*, Trevor. Not dirty clothes."

FOUND IN LIBBY'S SKETCHPAD

My Friend Trevor - Not So Daring

HOLA!
Kitty Cat!

Trevor dropped his head. "Fine. You win."

Libby took a breath and patted him on the shoulder. "Okay, then. Maybe it's time you loosened up on that rule. Open up to some change."

A loud scraping sound at the door caught Trevor's attention. He looked over and saw one of the remodel workers entering the building, dragging a fake palm tree and a hammock. Trevor spun back around and faced Libby. "Palm trees and hammocks? Really? Don't you think that's a little *too* much change?"

"It's just what Kip said. We should be comfortable *and* look good. I happen to agree with that," she said.

Having been dismissed from the assembly—since Trevor and Libby didn't seem to be returning any time soon—the students suddenly spilled out into the hallway. Libby motioned for Trevor to follow her over to a corner—the spot where the crew worker had placed the fake palm tree.

"Here's the truth," she said in a quiet voice. "This is my chance to leave a legacy at this school—change it for the better. Forever. I want to be a different kind of class president, to stand out." She reached out and grabbed his arm. "I don't want to be ordinary, Trevor. That's the reason why I'm doing this. So I decided to think big, just like you told me."

Trevor decided it was time to give her the whole truth. "I can't do it, Libby. I'm getting art lessons from Mr. Jeffries at lunch. And I invited Molly."

Libby couldn't believe it. She had assumed he would be just as excited about winning this school makeover as she was, but it was clear she was wrong. He'd rather spend his lunch drawing. With Molly?

Ouch.

But Libby was determined to work with Kip Lee no matter what. This was no time to let disappointments get in the way.

"Forget about it," she said. "I'll find another partner."

Trevor watched as she bounced down the hallway. He thought it was kind of cool that even after he told her he wouldn't help out, she still had a spring in her step.

But then he noticed something strange. Something . . . different. The groups of kids passing by didn't keep walking. They stopped and talked to Libby. They asked her about the makeover. She pulled out some sketches of ideas she planned to share with Kip. The crowd around her grew bigger and bigger. She was beaming with excitement. And so was everyone else. Trevor could tell she was finally feeling anything but ordinary.

That moment hit him like a hammer over the head. Sometimes a smile on your friend's face is worth a change in your personal life policy.

"Libby, wait up!" he called after her. "I changed my mind."

Libby Gardner

Next to a fake
palm, pleasantly
surprised

11:30 a.m.

I'm not sure why Trevor changed his mind. I'm guessing he was really moved by my speech about leaving a legacy here at Westside. It was pretty good, if I say so myself.

But honestly, the thing I didn't tell him was that . . . well . . . this is sort of embarrassing . . . but the truth is that everyone thinks me winning that contest and getting Kip Lee to come to our school is the COOLEST thing ever. And people I don't even KNOW are sharing their ideas and saying nice things to me. But most important?

[clasps her hands together and takes a deep breath]

Savannah Maxwell! She's the most awesome, perfect, smartest, popular eighth grade girl here. She was elected their class president, and she walked up to me . . . ME . . . and said she wanted to talk to me about the show. We're meeting at lunch today to discuss it. And when she walked off, she even said, "See you later, Libby," as she twirled away from me.

That's right. Savannah Maxwell said my name mid-twirl . . . IN MY PRESENCE.

This is huge! Becoming besties with the eighth grade president could launch my popularity into the stratosphere! I'm finally going to stand out.

I just have to make sure this makeover goes PERFECTLY.

Trevor Jones

Standing near the
nurse's office,
fidgety

11:31 a.m.

I never did make it into the nurse's office again to
see if that washcloth works for personal problems.
Not good. Because I DEFINITELY need to find a way
to fix this.

See, I'm glad I told Libby I'd be on the design
team with her. That seemed like the right thing to do.

But now I can't hang out in the art room with
Molly during lunch. And she's going to be upset
with me for choosing Libby instead of her. So
maybe it was the wrong thing to do. I have no idea
how people make the right decisions all the time.
Is that even possible?!

[stuffs hands in pockets]

I guess the first thing I'll do is explain to
Mr. Jeffries why I won't be there at lunch for a
couple of weeks. Teachers always understand. It's
part of their job description, I think.

And then I'll get some guts to tell Molly.
Somehow.

Marty Nelson

Still looking
confused

11:32 a.m.

I still don't get it. Decker kept saying the word
MAKEOVER during the assembly, and I still never
figured out exactly what that means.

And then that super-tan guy did a LOT of pacing
around, and I got sort of dizzy. But I have to
say that tanning thing might just be a good idea.
Camouflage.

I'm going to look into this.

CHAPTER SIX

LUNCHTIME. **L**IBBY WAS EXCITED TO EAT HER LUNCH with Savannah, in public, where others would actually see them. Her reputation was about to shoot through the roof. The awesomeness of this day was ranking right up there with her tenth birthday.

$50 Gift Certificate to The Organizational Container Store!

Presented to: *Libby Gardner* on her 10th Birthday! $50

Congratulations on receiving your FIRST issue of:

Li'l Politician Magazine

LIBBY'S TENTH-BIRTHDAY GIFTS

Just before Libby reached the cafeteria doors, she heard someone call out to her.

"Libby—over here!"

It was Savannah Maxwell, motioning for her to join her down the empty hall.

Libby wondered why they weren't meeting at one of the tables. Didn't lunch together mean lunch . . . in the lunch-room . . . eating lunch?

Maybe Savannah wants us to make an entrance together, Libby thought. Cool girls know how to make an entrance.

Libby quickly fluffed her hair and rushed over to her. "Savannah! Hi! I love your boots! And your shirt! And your hair!" *Wow, I'm rambling. Keep your cool.*

Libby took a quick breath to calm down. "Did . . . did you want to talk about the school makeover?"

"Yep." Savannah narrowed her eyes. "What's your problem, Libby? Why didn't you come tell *me* about it first?"

Libby stepped back, shocked by her tone. Was she mad? This made no sense—she'd been perfectly delightful earlier in the day. "I just wanted it to be a surprise for the school," Libby tried to explain.

"A surprise?! I'm the eighth grade class president, and now I look like a fool for not being a part of any of this."

Oh, no. This can't be happening. Libby nervously gripped

the hem of her shirt. "I'm so sorry, Savannah. I'll make it up to you. I'll talk to Kip about getting you on the design team, too."

"Forget it. I don't think we'll be doing *any* projects together, Libby." Savannah threw her hair over her shoulder and marched past her.

Libby's bottom lip quivered. She'd never intended to upset her. Surely there was a way to work this out. "Savannah, please!" she called out after her. "Anything you want. I'll talk to Kip. We'll work it out!"

Savannah and her quite-nice boots came to a complete stop. She slowly turned back to face Libby. "Anything I want?"

Libby nodded. "Anything."

Savannah took a few steps closer. "Well, there is *one* thing I'd like."

"Whatever it is . . . I'll do it." Libby smiled at her. Score! She'd managed to turn Savannah Maxwell back around. Libby knew that buddying up with her would send her popularity soaring. No more basic respect from her peers—she'd finally be the one who was asked to sit with all the right people at lunch. And maybe, just maybe . . . she'd start to have a busy weekend social life.

Today—this moment—would be what started it all.

* * *

Trevor's talk with Mr. Jeffries went very well. As he'd expected, teachers could be quite understanding. When Trevor told him he couldn't meet at lunch for drawing lessons since he was on the makeover team, Mr. J smiled, nodded, and said, "No worries."

So easy! Trevor thought. If only this conversation I'm about to have with Molly could go as smoothly.

While Trevor waited in the lunch line, he felt a tap on the shoulder.

"Is it true?" Marty, his eighth grade friend from down the street, had walked up next to him. Marty had a freshly shaved head, a rolled-up copy of the newest edition of *Extreme Catfishing* in his back pocket, and a big grin on his face.

"Yes, Marty," Trevor said. "It's mashed-potato day. Your favorite day of the week."

"Not that. I heard you changed your mind after that big I-have-a-headache scene at the assembly. You're going to help with the makeover with Libby and that Hollywood guy—true?"

"Next!" the lunch lady called out.

"Nuggets. Corn. Mashed potatoes, no gravy," Trevor explained to her. "Thanks, Mrs. Longfellow." He turned back to Marty. "And yes, it's true, I'm helping Libby out. Everyone seems excited about the makeover, and I'm starting this new thing where I'm open to change." He peeked over the counter. "PLEASE, no gravy!" Trevor grabbed his tray from the lunch lady, disappointed. He showed it to Marty. "Look. Gravy."

"I thought you were opening up to change."

"Next!"

"Double potatoes, double gravy," Marty said, then turned to Trevor. "Here's the deal. Let's not say the word *makeover*. I can't figure out what it means. And also, it's weird." Marty grabbed his lunch tray, filled with exactly what he'd ordered, and motioned for Trevor to follow him over to the salad bar. He filled a bowl with the same ingredients he did every single day: hard-boiled eggs, shredded cheese, bacon bits, olives, ranch dressing, and more bacon bits.

"No lettuce?" Trevor asked.

"I like to get right to the point."

Marty topped off his salad with croutons and said, "Please tell me this makeov—I mean, *change* to the school, will not take away my salad bar. Especially the bacon bits— there are never enough."

Trevor wasn't really sure how to answer him. He had no

idea what Kip's plans were, so it was entirely possible many things were going to change. He couldn't make Marty any promises . . . but he could promise to try.

"I don't know what Kip has planned, but Libby and I *are* a part of the design team now. I'm sure we'll have some say in what gets done. I'll do my best to save your salad bar."

"And the bacon bits?"

"Priority number one."

Marty scratched his ear, thinking this over. If Trevor could help save his precious salad bar, maybe he could do other things? Because just that morning, Marty had read an article online that stated there was a 74 percent higher chance of slipping on wet tile than any other material. Instantly Marty had thought of the boys' locker room. All tile. Accidents were just waiting to happen!

"There is one more thing, actually."

"Like what?" Trevor squinted at him.

"Rugs. We need a couple of indoor/outdoor rugs in the locker room. It will reduce the rate of slipping. It's a safety issue, Trevor. Talk to that Hollywood guy, would you?"

"Okay, okay—calm down. Your gravy is about to spill. Libby and I meet with him in a few minutes, after we eat. I'll talk to him about getting your rugs."

"Thanks, Trevor. This makeover may not be so bad after all." Marty headed off to the eighth grade section.

Trevor noted how readily Marty used the word *makeover* now without having a pukey look on his face. So strange. It seemed like *everyone* was getting excited about this remodel.

Everyone except for one person.

Across the room, Trevor saw Molly hunched over her lunch tray, poking at her chicken nuggets. He slid into the seat next to her. "Nugget hockey?"

"No," she said, but her voice was so low, Trevor could barely hear her.

Molly didn't want to admit she actually *was* playing chicken nugget hockey. Mostly because she didn't want to make eye contact with him. If he saw her face, he might actually see that her feelings were hurt. Trevor seemed to have a way of noticing when something was wrong, even when she didn't tell him. She wouldn't let him figure it out today, though.

Trevor leaned in. "What's wrong, Molly?"

She threw her hands in the air. "How did you know something was wrong? I didn't even make eye contact!"

He looked down. "The picture you drew on your napkin."

Molly dropped her head. "Oh."

"I'm sorry about not hanging out in the art room with you at lunch. But there's still half an hour left. You should just go by yourself." Trevor was trying to be helpful, but when the words came out, he realized they didn't sound so nice.

Molly looked up at him but didn't say anything. She

Something's
Wrong

FOUND ON MOLLY'S NAPKIN

wished he would just change his mind again. Trevor was friends with her *and* Libby, except Molly couldn't help but notice that he always chose Libby.

"You're right," she said. "I'm better off by myself. Always have been."

"That's not what I meant—"

"I think what you meant to say was you'd rather decorate the school with Libby than draw with me. I get it."

"No, it's not like I *want* to help Kip Lee out. I don't want to do anything with that guy, honestly." He sighed and dropped his head. "It's all so . . . difficult sometimes."

"Look, if you don't want to do something, then don't. If you do, then do. Why does life seem so simple to me all the time?"

Just then, Libby rushed up to them, clipboard in hand. "Trevor, we have to head to the library—it's time for our first planning meeting!"

Trevor looked over at Molly and cringed like she was a firecracker with a lit fuse. "Talk to you later?" She didn't respond; she just passed a piece of corn to her left-wing chicken nugget.

Since he couldn't get another word out of Molly, Trevor joined Libby and headed toward the library. He figured this walk would probably be the best time to mention that he promised Marty he'd ask Kip for that favor.

"Libby, I need to tell you something."

Trevor explained all about the favor to Marty—the rugs, the bacon bits. He fully expected a lecture from Libby on how you shouldn't promise things to people unless you knew you could come through for them and blah, blah, blah.

Instead, Libby smirked and said, "I promised Savannah Maxwell full-length mirrors in the girls' locker room."

"You what?!"

"She said it's too difficult to see if an *entire* outfit is working with only the mirrors over the sinks." Libby kept power walking while Trevor struggled to keep up. "That all sounds pretty reasonable to me, Trev. I *have* to convince Kip to get those mirrors."

"It sounds like you're just trying to impress Savannah Maxwell."

"Well, so what? What's the difference? You're doing the same thing with Marty. At least we're gaining friends, not losing them."

As Trevor opened the library door to let Libby in, he said under his breath, "Let's hope so."

Molly Decker

In the lunchroom, throwing away her mutilated chicken nuggets

12:20 p.m.

Whatever. I don't care—Trevor can go remodel the school ALL HE WANTS. It's just more art time for me.

But the guy's just making his life difficult when it doesn't have to be. Who DOES that?

Maybe I need to show him that making decisions CAN be simple.

[starts hunting around in her backpack]

But right now I'm going to look for some crackers, because I'm starving. I played WAY too much hockey during lunch and never ate my food.

Corey Long

Holding a notebook.
Unusual, no matter
the time of day

12:21 p.m.

So that Kip guy hasn't asked me a single question about my hair. Weird.

But then again . . . I've been pretty busy today. I'm working on my latest masterpiece. Just don't tell ANYONE.

[looks left, then right]

I've been making my own tell-all piece. It's a comic book, and it shows the funny side of life here at Westside. Along with some exaggeration and then some stuff that blows up. IT'S SICK, BRO!

Yeah, I love to draw.

[cringes]

I can't believe I just admitted that out loud. Edit that part out, man.

CHAPTER SEVEN

AS THEY STOOD AT THE ENTRANCE TO THE LIBRARY, Libby and Trevor froze in disbelief at what they were seeing. Next to Kip Lee, propped up on a rolling cart, was a slushee machine. A super-sleek, state-of-the-art slushee machine with the logo of the show on the front of it, blinking in neon lights.

"Well? What do you think?" Kip asked as he poured a small sample of a blue ice drink for himself.

Libby glared at the machine, then at Trevor, then back at Kip. "ITISAWESOME!" she blurted, quite loudly.

But Trevor wasn't so sure about the awesomeness of it, or the need to blurt it out in a shouting manner. "But Mr. Lee, we're in school. And this is a *library*. I don't think Vice Principal Decker will allow this." Trevor looked past

the slushee machine and saw Mrs. Shulman, the librarian, behind her desk shaking her head and fanning herself with a pad of Post-it notes. Clearly, she was not too happy with this situation.

Kip swallowed his frozen blueberry drink and laughed. "It's not going to stay in here. We're hiding it until we can roll it into the cafeteria to surprise the kids. Lunch will be over in about twenty minutes, so we need to get in there pronto."

Libby shifted her clipboard over to the other hand and pulled a pen out to take notes. "I'm sure I can find the perfect corner for it, Mr. Lee."

"But why a frozen drink machine?" Trevor asked. "I thought you'd do things like give us chairs and a fresh coat of paint."

Kip casually took another sip and said, "Well, the show *is* called *Trick Out My School*. Putting a slushee machine in the cafeteria will make the kids happy. That way we can go about our work without any complaints. It just works better this way if—aaaaahh! Brain freeze!"

While he pushed on his head to get the pain out, Trevor leaned over to Libby and whispered, "Complaints? About what?"

She shrugged.

"Whew, it's gone," Kip said. "Anyway, let me show you some of my plans for the school." He unrolled his blueprint and showed them exactly what he had in store for Westside.

- New paint in the hallways
- Beanbags in the library

- Nightclub dining in the cafeteria (chaise lounges, large disco ball)
- Bali-inspired relaxation area in the lobby (with water feature)
- Surround-sound system installed throughout the school (for students to play music of their choice between classes)
- Flowing chocolate-milk fountain
- Bowling-themed boys' bathroom (must knock down pins to get the dispenser to roll out a paper towel)
- Movie-themed girls' bathroom (must choose "Which movie was best?" from a touch screen before entering a stall)

Libby's eyes grew big and filled with excitement—this was just too much! She had known they'd get a school makeover, but this was a lifestyle change!

Trevor leaned over to get a good look at Kip's list, and his eyes also grew big, but they were *not* filled with excitement. All this change was too much. He actually liked the chairs in the library—they provided terrific back support. And the tables in the cafeteria were quite easy to clean off. How were they supposed to eat on lounge chairs? He had promised Libby he was going to be the new "Totally

Open to Change Trevor Jones," but now just looking at the blueprints for change was making him queasy.

But he'd promised Marty bacon bits and rugs, so he shook off the icky feelings. And he had to admit . . . a bowling-themed bathroom was pretty cool. Also, the chocolate-milk fountain. Also, well . . . just about all of it. "It's a great list," Trevor said. "But Libby and I have some ideas to add to it."

"Ideas. Great."

Trevor was relieved Kip was willing to listen to their suggestions. Maybe this guy wasn't so bad after all. "We could use rugs in the boys' locker room—to increase safety," Trevor said.

Then Libby joined in. "And we definitely would like full-length mirrors in the girls' bathroom."

"Also, please keep the salad bar, and add extra bacon bits," Trevor said. "Oh! And install electric pencil sharpeners." He figured while they were asking for favors, he'd ask for one of his own, too.

"Interesting ideas, kids," Kip said. Then he turned to a cameraman who was standing over in nonfiction. "Cut! Did you get all that, Al?"

"You bet," Al replied, then started putting his camera away.

"You were recording that?!" Libby clasped her hands together and bounced on her toes.

Kip double-checked his necklace, making sure it was slightly off balance. It took a lot of effort to maintain his look of sloppy-perfect. "Of course we were filming. We always like to include footage of us explaining to the students what we're going to do with the remodel."

"This is amazing!" Libby turned and whispered to Trevor, "Did my hair look okay?"

"Of course." Then he secretly checked to make sure he didn't have any chicken nugget in his teeth.

Kip Lee

Readjusting his
necklace

12:40 p.m.

I have to admit it's a little strange talking to
a different camera crew. I'm used to my own—they
know my best angles.

But anyway, sure, I listen to the kids when
they have design ideas. At almost EVERY school,
the students have asked for electric pencil sharpeners. And bacon bits. So I'm not surprised by
their requests.

But right now I need to find out if there's a
place in this town where I can get a decent latte.
And I might starve if I can't find some good sushi.

[shakes head]

No one seems to get how difficult my job is.

Kip Lee's camera guy

On break, drinking a Diet Coke

12:41 p.m.

Bro! Good to see you, man. Remember when we worked together on that *Househusbands of Houston* show? Good times.

But now we're following around Kip Lee. Just be careful when you're filming him—ALWAYS film from his left, and never film too early in the morning, before he's had a latte.

PLEASE tell me there's a place in this town to get a decent latte. And good cell phone reception.

Honestly, bro—this town is already driving me a little nuts. Even my dog is bored.

CHAPTER EIGHT

AFTER THE CAMERAS HAD BEEN TURNED OFF, LIBBY realized Kip hadn't said much about their remodeling ideas yet.

Using her sweetest, most persuasive voice, Libby said, "So . . . Mr. Lee. Can we get back to talking about our remodeling ideas? Trevor and I were thinking that—"

"Great," Kip interrupted. "But not now. First we need to get this slushee machine down to the cafeteria." He yanked on the rolling cart and started to push.

Trevor stepped forward. "Let me help you with that."

Kip shook his head. "No. By 'we,' I mean *my* team will take it down there. This requires lots of strength. You two stay here, unpack these boxes, and vacuum."

Libby gave him a thumbs-up. "Don't worry, we're on it!"

The crew took hold of the machine and backed out of the library door while Kip directed. Just before he stepped out, Kip turned back and said, "One more thing." He pointed at Trevor. "Move all those nonfiction books out of the way to another section. We need the room for the new reading area—the Library Lounge-o-Rama. Thanks, Taylor."

"My name is Trevor," he tried to correct him, but Kip had already left.

Libby walked over to him and patted him on the back. "Don't worry. If you want, I can help you with those books, Taylor," she joked.

"Funny."

"Oh, come on. You kind of look like a Taylor."

"What exactly does a Taylor look like?"

She smirked. "Brilliant. Helpful. Superstrong. The kind of guy who moves books all by himself. Have fun!" Libby danced off toward the boxes in the corner and started to open them.

Trevor picked up a stack of books, then added a couple more due to his awesome strength. *Maybe my mom should have named me Taylor*, he thought. But deep down, he knew he was *all Trevor*.

"Working hard?" Cindy Applegate had suddenly

Trevor —(n.) name given to those prone to utter humiliation.

appeared in the library. And strangely, she was holding a steaming-hot to-go cup of coffee.

"What's that for?" Libby dropped her box and walked up to her.

"A surprise for Kip! I called my mother during lunch and had her bring it up to the school. It's a vanilla latte with caramel topping and extra whip. He's going to love it! Then maybe we can talk about some of my design ideas. Where is he?"

Libby stuck her hand on her hip. "He's doing something in the cafeteria right now. But you can leave it here. I'll be sure he gets it."

Cindy waved her off. "Nah! You're so busy with all those dirty boxes. I'll go give it to him myself. Toodles!" Cindy turned and skipped away without spilling even a drop of the vanilla latte.

Trevor looked over to Libby. "Tell me she didn't just say *toodles*. I can't handle that being a thing now."

But Libby was worried about something else. "Trevor, what if he's impressed with her?"

"*Her?*"

"What if he listens to her design ideas or something? I mean, *I'm* the one who's been studying design since I was a little kid. Cindy just puts ribbon on things and calls herself an expert. She doesn't study design; she just Googles her favorite words."

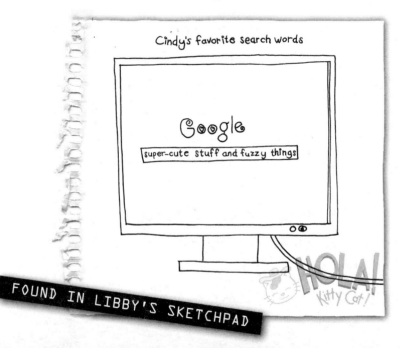

Cindy's favorite search words

Google

super-cute stuff and fuzzy things

HOLA!
Kitty Cat!

FOUND IN LIBBY'S SKETCHPAD

"Don't worry. I'm sure Kip will see right through her."

Libby smiled. "Thanks, Trev."

They got back to work unpacking the boxes. One contained a shag rug and new lamps—totally modern, with crystals hanging off the lamp shades. Then they came to a box labeled chairs, but they weren't heavy at all. Libby pulled back a flap and peered in. "Aha! Beanbags!" She pulled out one that was cherry red and another in zebra print.

The fact that they were now going to be able to sit on beanbags in the library was almost too cool to believe. All that comfort . . . at school!

They set out the beanbags next to each other and plopped down to relax. Trevor, though, was fairly certain his was missing a bean or two.

"Not sure how I'm going to read in here," Trevor said, his voice muffled.

"Quit playing around. Kip will be back soon." Libby looked up to see the library door opening. *Soon* meant *now*. Grabbing Trevor by the hand, she yanked him out of his beanbag cocoon. "We're finished, Mr. Lee!" Libby spread her arms out as if this were a display on a game show. "What do you think?"

But Kip didn't look their way and didn't even seem to notice Libby had asked a question with a flourish. He

was too busy talking to Cindy, who was trailing just inches behind him.

"Listen carefully. I drink nonfat skinny lattes. Two fake sugars. None of that real sugar. It makes me bloat like a toad."

Cindy took notes on the palm of her hand using her pink gel pen. "Nonfat . . . bloat . . . like . . . toad. Got it!"

"Oh, and while you're at it, I need some sushi. Yellow-tail tuna. Spicy. Extra avocado. Dipped in sesame seeds. I want it with brown rice, not white." He halted and whirled around to get a good look at her. "What's your name?"

She looked up at him, her eyes twinkling. "Cindy. Cindy Applegate!"

"Brown rice, Cindy-Cindy. Do *not* come near me with white rice, or I will swell up like a water balloon." He placed his hand on her shoulder. "Can you do this for me?"

She raised an eyebrow. "Every designer needs a protégé. I'm your girl. Brown rice, no matter what."

"You may have potential." He turned and looked over at Libby and Trevor. "Are you listening to this, Libby and Toby?"

Libby wasn't sure how to respond. "What . . . what do you mean?"

"You get ahead by *doing*, not questioning."

Libby thought they were going to talk about her ideas, but it looked like following orders was more what he was looking for. Maybe *then* he'd listen to ideas? But when it came to following orders, it looked like Cindy had already beaten her to the punch.

"I'll see you after school with some supplies!" Cindy waved as she walked off. "Toodles!"

Oh, no, Trevor thought. Toodles *is* a thing now.

Kip waved at her. "Cindy-Cindy is so helpful."

Libby dropped her shoulders. *Helpful*: that was a word she never expected to hear in a sentence with Cindy's name.

But Libby was determined to find a way to impress Kip Lee.

And she wasn't about to let Cindy-Cindy get in the way.

Libby Gardner

Pacing outside the
library, slightly
agitated

12:59 p.m.

Cindy making TOODLES a "thing" isn't my biggest
problem. Though it's highly irritating—I can see
Trevor's point. No, my biggest problem is that Kip
is already impressed with her, and he didn't say
a WORD about the work Trevor and I did.

But I still need to make sure he listens to me
about the mirrors Savannah wants. I promised her—
and a politician always keeps her promises.

Plus I was hoping to show him some of my design
boards and swatches to see if he likes my ideas. I
need an honest critique of my skills to see if inte-
rior designer is truly my calling. You know . . .
after my political career as a senator.

But for now, if the best way to get his attention is through good food, then I can do that.

In fact, I'll go a step further.

And Cindy will never see this coming.

Molly Decker

Standing outside
the girls'
bathroom, highly
annoyed

1:00 p.m.

It's only Day One, and I can't take this anymore.
When I tried to go to stall number four—my Thinking Stall—I saw the bathroom was closed because
the workers were in there painting. There was
a LOT of good stuff sketched on those bathroom
walls. I can't think without walls of graffiti
surrounding me.

[huffs]

[twice]

I was used to the way things were around here.
Squeaky chairs, bad lighting, lockers painted the
color of throw-up. It was comforting. And now
THIS?!

I have to find a way to stop the makeover.
There HAS to be a way.

WESTSIDE
MIDDLE SCHOOL

MAKEOVER
DAY TWO

CHAPTER NINE

THE NEXT DAY, TREVOR FOUND HIMSELF IN THE HALLWAY with a paintbrush in his hand applying a coat of green paint to the walls. Kip kept reminding him, however, that the paint was *not* green. It was Sea Salt Reflection—a combination of teal and mint and crushed seashells.

Not the color of seashells. Actual. Crushed. Seashells.

Which Trevor had to admit was completely rad. He leaned in to see if he could hear the sounds of the ocean. Which would be even radder, if such a word existed. But it didn't work—no ocean sounds.

"Hi, Trevor!"

He looked over his shoulder and saw Jamie Jennison along with her best friend, Becca Bolton (a.k.a. Becca with

Braces), standing behind him. Trevor assumed they became best friends because both of their parents were clearly fond of alliteration.

Trevor set his brush down. "What's up?"

Jamie leaned in closer. "That's so cool you're on the makeover team. Could you do us a favor?" She flashed a big, persuasive smile.

"Sure."

"Becca and I *really* want a new volleyball court outside. Maybe with real sand and everything! Would you mind asking Kip for us?"

"Oh, oh!" Becca started bouncing on her toes. "And could you ask him to paint our lockers a new color? They're hideous—rodent colored. Maybe he could paint them pink? Or purple? Or POLKA DOTS! That'd be so awesome!"

Wow, Trevor thought. They're acting like I'm someone important. This is very tolerable.

Trevor batted his eyes. "Of course, ladies. I'll talk to him for you."

"Aw, thanks, Trevor!" Jamie and Becca skipped off down the hallway.

At that moment, Trevor realized this makeover might be his ticket to high-level popularity. And even if he had to find a way to remain cool after the makeover ended, it might be worth the risk. He'd finally get chosen first in kickball. And maybe he'd have the pick of any table at lunch. Not to mention he could end up with a favorable title in the yearbook. Last year in elementary school, he was voted "Most Likely to Always Be Here" due to his impeccable attendance rate. This year, though, he was hoping to get somewhere close to Corey's status.

Jose Lane
Kindest

Corey Long
Full of Awesome

Tabby Lowe
Perkiest Ponytail

FROM THE ARCHIVES

But he had a long way to go.

As Jamie and Becca headed down the hallway, Trevor noticed something. At the far end of the hall, someone else was painting as well. Not Kip, not Libby, not a crew worker. He rubbed his eyes to make sure he was really seeing what he was seeing: it was Corey Long with his own bucket of Sea Salt Reflection, eagerly painting the wall. Trevor's mouth dropped. What was going on?!

Corey looked up and noticed Trevor glaring, his jaw almost on the floor. He set his paintbrush down and strolled over to him. He figured Trevor would want to know what he was doing. And telling him Kip had personally picked him to join the design team sounded like a lot of fun.

"You dropped your jaw, Trevor," he said.

Trevor closed his mouth and didn't say anything; he just shot him a confused look.

"Kip wanted me to be on the design team," Corey explained. "He's taking me under his wing, I guess you could say."

Trevor didn't really care whose wing he was under; he just wanted Corey to be far away from him—especially when he was in the vicinity of a wet paintbrush. "How about you stay on your end and I'll stay on mine," Trevor suggested.

Corey shrugged. "No problem." He sauntered back over to his spot, satisfied that he'd probably made Trevor jealous. Making people jealous was one of his favorite activities.

Trevor went back to work, but within moments he felt a tap on the shoulder. Luckily it wasn't Corey. "Trevor, I have something to show you," Molly said.

He carefully placed his paintbrush on his drop cloth and turned to her. "What's up?" A smile filled his face because he was surprised—and very relieved—to see that Molly was finally talking to him again.

She pulled out a stack of papers from her backpack and shoved them into his hand. "I'm here to bust you out. Set you free."

He glanced down at the papers. "You're giving me paperwork with very small writing?"

She nodded energetically. If Trevor wasn't mistaken, there was even a sparkle in her eye. An excitement sparkle. So peculiar.

She shifted from foot to foot, unable to stand still. "See, last night I went onto the Web site for *Trick Out My School*, and I read all the rules and regulations." She looked around and lowered her voice. "Wait, where is Libby anyway?"

"She went to find Kip. Something about impressing him and Cindy never seeing this coming. Something like that. Anyway, go on."

"Last night, I tried to convince my dad to stop this

ridiculous makeover. But he wouldn't do it. Said he's far too excited about the office remodel Kip's doing for him—matching wingback chairs and everything. But guess what?" Molly didn't actually wait for him to guess what. "On the *Trick Out My School* Web site, in section four under 'Grievances,' it says that if the majority of the student body is unhappy with the remodel, they can sign a petition and it will . . . " She paused to look down at some notes she had scribbled on the palm of her hand. "It will stop the production and the right to air the program." The note actually went halfway up her arm.

Molly looked at Trevor. "That paper you're holding is a petition—all we have to do is fill it with signatures and this nightmare is over. Cool, right?!"

Trevor stood there blinking at her, unsure how to answer. Certainly he was relieved she was talking to him again. And it was intriguing—if not shocking—to see her this excited about paperwork. But *end* the makeover? That would just upset Libby, not to mention the rest of the school. Plus he'd already made promises to Marty and Jamie and Becca—promises that could get him an awesome tagline in the yearbook. He took a deep breath and told her the truth. "Molly, I don't want to stop the makeover."

"But earlier you said you didn't want to do it."

"It's true I can't stand loud hammering sounds, and I'm hesitant to accept change, but—"

She threw her hands in the air. "But what? They've already invaded my Thinking Stall, Trevor!"

He lowered his voice, trying to calm her down. "Listen, I know I said I wasn't excited about this, and I'm sorry about your stall, but—"

"But you'd rather do whatever *Libby* wants, is that it?"

"No, it's just that I'm starting to like the idea of making some changes. It might do me some good." He pointed at the wall. "I mean, look at this shade of green. Have you ever seen a color this awesome? There are actual seashells in there."

Molly did not take a moment to admire the green color or lean in to see if she could hear the ocean. Instead, she snatched the papers back from him. "This is a middle school, not a five-star resort. I give up. You and Libby have fun." She took off down the hall and disappeared into a crowd of students.

Trevor wondered if there would ever be a day when *both* Libby and Molly were talking to him. Couldn't the three of them ever agree on something? Maybe even get along?

But it was starting to seem like that day might never come.

Corey Long

Worried, hair
slightly floppy

12:59 p.m.

Okay, so TECHNICALLY Kip didn't personally pick me out to be on the design team. Being technical is such a drag, man.

But fine. Here's the deal: my mom's hairdresser has a cousin who knows the chiropractor of Kip Lee's dog groomer. So Mom asked for a favor and bam! Kip agreed to include me on the design team. Mom thinks this will launch my acting/reality TV career.

But this is the LAST thing I want to be doing. I need to find my comic book. It's missing—I can't find it ANYWHERE. It's important I get it back because I was working on this pivotal scene where Mr. Everett finds a werewolf in Wilson's closet, and there's this stick of dynamite and . . . oh, it's too complicated to explain.

Just keep your eye out for it, would you?

Libby stood outside Kip Lee's trailer door and prepared herself before she knocked. She tied her shoe. Checked her teeth. And stood up tall. It was true she was nervous, but Libby was confident that what she was about to give Kip would impress him far more than any latte Cindy could bring him.

Thoughtfulness. Research. Alphabetical folder tabs—that's what people like, Libby reminded herself.

Just as she raised her hand to knock on his trailer door, Kip opened it and hopped out. "Whatcha need, Libby? I was on my way to oversee the installation of the meditation water fountain in the lobby. Let's do a walk 'n' talk."

"Walk 'n' talk. Sure." Libby power walked next to him to keep up, and simultaneously pulled out a bag from her backpack. "First, I have some things for you. This is a bag of organic dark-chocolate espresso beans. Made daily at five thirty a.m. by our town's only coffee roaster. I picked these up this morning. In the dark."

He snatched the bag and continued speed walking. "Cool. Thanks."

"Also, there's this." Libby pulled out a three-ring binder from her backpack. "I made this for you. Since you have to spend two weeks in our town, I figured you and your crew

would want the best of everything. So I made a list, organized with color-coded tabs. And alphabetized, of course. There are restaurants, gas stations, and trinket shops where you can get a new key chain or visor hat. I even included mileage and consumer reviews. Also I drew stars on a map where our local celebrities live. They're not Hollywood types, but we're proud. Like Mrs. Duncan on Cottonwood Lane, who was once interviewed on CNN for a story about people who hoard newspapers. Everyone knows her now!"

Kip stopped at once, pointing to Mr. Nelson's star on the map. Libby almost tripped over Kip's feet. "I love cat swimming. This is just . . . impressive, Libby! Thank you so much!"

He walked on and waved at her. Libby stood frozen on the blacktop while her stomach did a triple somersault. She'd done it. Kip Lee had used her name and the word *impressive* together in the same sentence. Libby wished she had a calendar nearby because this day needed to be immediately decorated.

30	31	1	2 Annual Closet Re-organization	3	4	5
6	7	8	9	10 New label maker arrives!	11	12 New Bacon-flavored ranch dressing comes out!
13	14 BEST DAY EVER! I meet Kip!!!	15 I impressed Kip! Best Day EVER!	16 Day after I impressed Kip	17 Day after the day after I impressed Kip	18	19
20	21	22	23	24	25	26
27	28	29	30	1	2	3

FOUND IN LIBBY'S CALENDAR

CHAPTER TEN

To SAY THAT TREVOR AND LIBBY SIMPLY "ASSISTED" with the makeover would be an understatement. They helped replace cabinets. Painted walls. Doors. Baseboards. They exchanged the bright overhead fluorescent lights in the library with "moodier" lower-watt bulbs. Libby teetered on a ladder to help install a large disco ball in the cafeteria. Trevor helped mount a flat-screen TV on the wall of the teachers' lounge. And they both helped with building the chocolate-milk fountain.

To put it simply: they worked like dogs.

Today, their job was to remove all the cafeteria chairs and replace them with chaise lounges.

Lunchtime at Westside was about to get swanky.

As Trevor and Libby dragged the last of the old chairs

outside, Trevor decided this was a good time to tell her his news: that Jamie and Becca weren't the only ones who put in makeover requests. "So, Lib? The Baker twins asked me to get XM radio in the boys' locker room." He then pulled out a piece of paper and read from the list he'd made. "And Nancy wants a weight-training room. And Jake Jacobs wants a skate ramp. And the entire baseball team asked for a batting cage. Also, new socks. So I told them . . ." He winced, hoping she wouldn't blow her top at this part. "I told them yes—that I'd ask Kip."

Strangely, Libby didn't launch into a lecture about promising favors. Or that socks aren't exactly part of a school makeover. Instead, she smiled and looked downright excited. "Mandy Weston asked me about getting a pastry bar. And the yearbook staff would like better cameras and Internet access." She laced her fingers together. "Can you believe it, Trevor? This makeover is launching our popularity into the solar system!"

He had to admit: He doubted it was a good idea at first. But now? Full of awesome. He smiled at her. "You'll definitely be our president in eighth grade, Lib."

She blushed. "And before you know it, you're going to get picked first at kickball."

As ridiculous of a life goal as that sounded, it totally was Trevor's dream. "Now all we have to do is pitch our ideas to Kip."

They looked around the cafeteria and saw Kip wandering around supervising all the workers. "We need a cozy atmosphere," Kip said as he sipped one of Cindy's lattes while she followed closely behind him. But she'd moved on

from simply bringing him coffee. When Cindy had heard about Libby's impressive list of places to visit around town, she upped her game in order to get noticed. "Twinsies" was what she called it.

Just then, Kip sent Cindy on an errand to find a Crescent wrench. It was obvious from the confused look on Cindy's face that she wouldn't be returning anytime soon. So Libby and Trevor decided it would be the perfect moment to talk to Kip about their remodeling ideas.

The two of them gave each other encouraging nods, knowing this talk was important. Libby *had* to get him to agree to all the things the students had requested—the most important one being the new mirrors she'd promised Savannah. It had been several days since their lunchtime discussion, and Libby needed to stay true to her word. This would guarantee a friendship with Savannah, which would guarantee Libby a political future. Which would all just be so cool. Also: where did Savannah get those boots? This was something Libby really needed to know.

While Trevor didn't care about a political career or footwear, he did know this talk with Kip was important. He had to get those indoor/outdoor rugs he'd promised Marty. At this stage of his middle school career, he simply couldn't afford to lose Marty as a friend for a single second. Most of his advice on how to survive middle school had come from him—Marty was his personal new Mystical 7 Ball. Actually, the Mystical 7 Ball had a bit of an attitude problem, so maybe Marty was even better.

"Kip? We have some ideas we'd like to share with you," Libby said as they slunk up to him.

He was busy scrolling down his phone. "Mmm-hmm," he replied without looking up.

Libby nudged Trevor with her elbow and pushed him forward, signaling he should go first.

But going first was not his favorite.

Trevor scratched his head and tried to pull together his best compelling argument. "So about those requests we made earlier . . . uh, see . . . according to page thirty-seven, or maybe it's page seventy-three, of *Boys' Life* magazine or possibly *Extreme Hunter* magazine, it says that it's dangerous to have water near tile floor when it's simultaneously near boys ages twelve to thirteen. So they suggest rugs. For safety. Um . . . and they can be camouflage color. Or not. Your choice."

Kip crinkled his forehead but just stared at his phone and didn't say anything.

So Libby stepped up and filled in the silence. "And in addition to Trevor's fantastic idea, I think we should include full-length mirrors in the girls' bathroom. Otherwise we may see an outbreak of horrible fashion ensembles that simply cannot be tolerated. We won't be able to focus on our academic studies with all that poor taste distracting us. Our grades will suffer, Mr. Lee!"

Oh, nice one, Trevor thought. I totally should have gone with the academic angle.

Kip looked up and studied their faces. Then finally he said, "You're asking for rugs? And mirrors?"

"Right," Libby said. "But there's more actually."

They both then went through their lists of requests from the students, even down to the new baseball socks.

Kip listened while he fidgeted with his hair, though it didn't move. "We're under a strict budget, kids. There's only so much I can do."

"Oh." Libby dropped her shoulders.

"But don't worry. I'll find a way to make it happen. Okay?" He whirled around and headed down the hall.

Libby and Trevor high-fived and said in unison, "Yes!"

The two then moved on to their next task of painting the library walls in the fiction section.

But it didn't take long before tempers flared.

Libby and Trevor were standing in AUTHORS M–Z when they heard all the yelling.

Wilson

Next to his
Supply Containment
Unit, quite annoyed

12:45 p.m.

There I was, just minding my own business, trying to calm down Savannah Maxwell. She was crying because she'd gotten her locker jammed. I tried explaining to her the physics of shoving a knee-length faux-fur coat into a two-by-two-by-four—foot space, but she was—without a doubt—hysterical. I decided it probably wasn't a good time to point out that it was sixty-four degrees outside and a sweater vest would've sufficed.

Instead, I immediately went to my Supply Containment Unit to retrieve Lefty, my locker de-jamming device.

And that's when I saw them. Kip Lee and his workers ripping out the shelves in my unit. I repeat: RIPPING them out. And those shelves were VERY important to me. They were left over from the building of Graceland—Elvis's home. I can't verify that, but that's what the seller on eBay claimed, and he had very high reviews, so there's no reason for me to doubt it.

Losing those shelves would be DISASTROUS. Not to mention the fact that I am now unable to quickly locate my tools in an emergency. Not that my organizational system was all that impressive, but at least it was MY organizational system. So, to answer your question, THAT is why I started yelling.

Kip Lee

Far away from
Wilson's Supply
Containment Unit,
feeling
unappreciated

12:48 p.m.

There I was, just minding my business, trying to take a few shelves out of the janitor's closet. Ripping out ugly shelving is one of my favorite parts of the job. VERY satisfying.

But when we looked around, we noticed everything was so oddly placed. No organization? Well, we won't have any of that at this school. All janitorial supplies will be organized by zones and color, which just makes SENSE.

So we got started, but the janitor barged in and started yelling. It's like he doesn't even appreciate our work. Ripping out old shelves is an art form.

CHAPTER ELEVEN

THE TWO MEN FACED EACH OTHER IN THE HALL OUTSIDE Wilson's Supply Containment Unit. There were a few minutes left before the end of lunch, so students were rushing by on the way to their lockers.

But once they heard Wilson's fury, a crowd quickly gathered. Wilson's anger, if not directed at you, was always enjoyable to witness.

"You have no right to rip down my shelves!"

"This is a school makeover. That includes your closet."

Wilson pointed to his sign. "It's a Supply Containment Unit."

"Fine. Your 'unit' was a disaster. Old shelves? No organization?"

Wilson narrowed his eyes. "It's organized by emergency.

Lefty, my locker tool, is always stored in the locker de-jamming section. Now I have no idea where it is!"

"What?!" Savannah Maxwell had stormed up to the gathered crowd, still sniffling. "But I have to get that coat out of my locker, or my mom will kill me. And I may have stashed my knee-high leather boots in there, too."

Several students yelled, "Savannah!" Because *everyone* knew all too well after multiple locker-safety trainings from Wilson that clunky clothes and accessories were not permitted in lockers. Otherwise, massive locker jammings. If there was anything Wilson was known for best, it was extensive student locker training.

"I'm sorry. Really! Please, can someone find that tool and help me out?" Savannah pleaded.

"Kip, here, reorganized, and now I don't know where it is," Wilson said.

Kip rolled his eyes. "What color is it?"

"Brown."

Kip sauntered over to the supply unit and returned with a box. He pointed to the label. "It's in the Medium Sized Brown Gadgets with Funny Looking Handles zone." He set the box down. "I'm organizing your stuff until we get your new shelves in place."

Wilson glanced over at the other labeled boxes. "So

you're saying all of my most precious supplies in the world are now in boxes organized in these *extremely* easy-to-understand zones. Is that correct?"

"Exactly."

Vice Principal Decker had heard all the commotion and charged up to them. "Is everything all right here? I heard shouting."

With the sudden appearance of the vice principal, all the kids quickly dispersed.

Wilson had a lot he wanted to say. That this remodel was not a good idea. That Westside didn't need all these changes. That he didn't like Kip Lee, not one bit.

But before he could start talking, Kip jumped in. "There's no problem here, Vice Principal Decker. Wilson and I now see eye-to-eye on this makeover. We're going to make this the most up-to-date closet—I mean, Supply Containment Unit—in the district. In fact, we're giving him brand-new replacement filters for his floor buffer. A hardworking man needs a floor buffer that works well." Kip patted Wilson on the back. "Sound good, friend?"

The last thing Wilson wanted was for Kip to think they were friends. But he really needed those filters. The last time he'd put in a request for them, he'd been denied. Not enough money in the budget.

Wilson hadn't been able to get a good shine on that floor in weeks. This school was due some ultra sparkling floors. The kids here deserve it, Wilson thought.

Forcing a smile, Wilson looked Kip over and said, "Thanks. We could use that." Then he reached into the box, grabbed Lefty, and set off down the hall to fix Savannah Maxwell's locker.

But he reminded himself to get a Pepto-Bismol tablet from the Stuff That Might Cause a Fire if Used Incorrectly box. Because his stomach was suddenly acting up.

Wilson always got a stomachache when there was something wrong.

Savannah Maxwell

Wearing a faux-fur coat and knee-high boots, feeling precious

1:00 p.m.

It's been a rough day. Fortunately, Wilson got my locker open, and I got my coat and boots. I also found two purses I hadn't seen in WEEKS, so my luck may be turning around.

Except I did go by the girls' bathroom several times today—or actually five or seven times—and they STILL haven't made the changes I asked for. No full-length mirrors. I can't possibly be expected to make outfit changes during the day without a proper full-length mirror.

Libby PROMISED she'd get Kip Lee to do it, but so far, she is not impressing me. As eighth grade class president, it looks like I'm going to have to take charge.

I need to have a talk with Mr. Lee myself.

Just as soon as I go shopping over the weekend—I'm in need of a new Asking for a Favor outfit.

WESTSIDE
MIDDLE SCHOOL
MAKEOVER
DAY EIGHT

CHAPTER TWELVE

THE FOLLOWING MONDAY, TREVOR ENTERED THE cafeteria at lunchtime and almost tripped over a trash can. The low lighting wasn't allowing for much visibility.

The Lunch Lounge—as it had been renamed—was now very similar to a dance club. (Minus the dance floor, but plus a bacon bar.)

Trevor's concerns over low lighting vanished when he heard his name being called out. And it wasn't coming from just one person . . . there were many people calling out his name, motioning for him to join them.

This is fantastic, Trevor thought. I can hardly see their faces, and I may trip over something any moment, but who cares? They're calling my name!

He decided to join Jamie Jennison and her group of friends. He set his drink down on the small (*extremely small*) coffee table and teetered his lunch tray on his knees. The lounge sofa didn't provide much support—in fact, he worried it might swallow him whole, just like that beanbag chair had in the library.

As he attempted to maintain his balance, Jamie and her friends fired away with questions.

"When are we getting the volleyball court?"

"And the polka-dot lockers?"

"And how about some new flavors in the slushee machine?"

Trevor leaned in, gripping his plate of spaghetti. "Don't worry. Kip's getting to it—I promise."

They nodded and continued. "And can we also get some lounge chairs to sit in while we wait in the car-pool line? It's exhausting out there."

"And some umbrellas to protect us from the sun?"

"Trevor, aren't you writing all this down?"

He nodded. "Uh . . . sure." He reached into his backpack, but in his attempt to grab a pen while simultaneously balancing spaghetti on his lap *and* looking very cool, he discovered the following: IT WASN'T POSSIBLE.

It was in that moment that he realized his new motto

of "being open to change" was going to be harder than he thought.

Much harder.

CHAPTER THIRTEEN

THE BUS RIDE HOME COULDN'T COME SOON ENOUGH. Except the bus ride was far from normal. Kip and his crew had gotten hold of the bus and tricked it out, too. Neon lights rimmed the ceiling, bamboo shades hung from the windows, and their seats now included drink holders and headrests.

It had never occurred to Trevor to trick out the bus. But honestly, only one word came to mind: ITISAWESOME!

Trevor considered telling Libby all about The Spaghetti Incident of a Few Hours Ago, but when he sat down next to her, he noticed she was happily writing in her notebook. He knew whenever she was writing this fast and this happily that he should save his story for later. Timing was everything with this girl.

He leaned over to get a peek. "What are you up to?" he asked.

She shielded her book. "Nothing."

But Trevor knew whenever Libby said "nothing," it always meant "something." Or more than likely: "something huge."

When they got off at their street, Trevor jogged up next to her to find out what was going on. Surely she'd answer, since she'd put her notebook away and was merely power walking.

"What was up with all the note taking on the bus?" he wheezed as he tried to keep up with her. Though Libby was only a couple of inches taller, her ability to walk/sprint made it seem as if she were twice his height.

"Like I said, it was nothing."

"Whenever you say 'nothing,' it actually means 'something.'" He looked around to see if there were volunteers handing out Gatorade, but no such luck. "And could you slow down? I'm winded, and there aren't any drink stations."

She paused and waited while he looked up at the sky, catching his breath. Finally, she said, "I'll tell you what I was writing, but you'll think I'm crazy."

Crazy? Trevor was intrigued. He raised a brow. "Go on."

"I know Kip said we should wait until the end of the week to see if he can work our ideas into the budget. But I can't just sit around and wait. Those neon lights on the bus are fabulous, and the headrests are ergonomically awesome. But I have to convince him to hurry up and do the mirrors in the bathroom for Savannah. I heard she had a bad day last week with her accessories getting stuck—that girl's been through enough already."

"You're talking about a girl whose definition of a bad day is getting her designer boots stuck in her locker for all of twelve minutes."

Libby stuck a hand on her hip. "She needs my help. I can't let her down." Libby headed down the street toward her house, but she briefly paused and looked back at Trevor, her face softening. "But if I need help with ideas, can I call you later?"

"Of course."

"And maybe you could call Molly, too. She's good at coming up with new ideas."

Trevor kicked at a rock. "Uh . . . see . . . she's not really talking to me right now."

"Why not?"

Trevor didn't want to tell her the real reason: That she hated the remodel. That Molly didn't want to lose the squeaky cafeteria chairs. Or her Thinking Stall. He also didn't want to make Libby mad by telling her Molly had gone on to the show's Web site to find a way to stop the makeover. Since Molly already wasn't speaking to him, there wasn't any sense in getting *everyone* mad at *everyone*. Being vague and peculiar was the only way to go here.

He scratched at his arm. "I think I'm allergic to having both of you being nice to me at the same time."

FOUND IN TREVOR'S NOTEBOOK

Double friendship = extreme hive victim

"Now you have allergies?" Libby narrowed her eyes, wondering if there was more to the story. "I'll call you later. Oh, and Trevor . . . why are there noodles in your shoe?"

He looked down. Darn! He had missed a couple of strands of spaghetti. Looking up at her, he blushed and said, "Uh . . . new trend?"

Trevor trudged into his house, wondering how he could say the right words so he'd someday have a week of friendship with both Libby and Molly. Even just a *day* of double friendship would be nice. He made a mental note to add it to his Christmas list.

Before he could even put down his backpack, the phone was ringing. Trevor answered quickly, hoping it wasn't someone from school pestering him about the makeover.

"When is Kip going to add extra bacon bits?"

He was wrong.

"Marty, I promise to talk to him tomorrow. He's been busy. But it will get done, don't worry."

"I like the drink holders on the bus, but it seems like a waste of money to me—bacon bits are much better."

"Of course, Marty." But Trevor wasn't sure that increasing bacon bits in the school cafeteria was such a good idea.

Trevor started to wonder if he should have made any promises at all. He needed to think this through. Weigh the consequences. Make some decisions. All that stuff that levelheaded people do.

For Trevor, getting his head level meant it was time for a talk with his mom.

Ms. Jones was in the kitchen organizing her drawer of candy.

"Can I have some chocolate candy, Mom? Or just one? Or five?"

"Of course not. You know I only allow sweets on Halloween or Easter. Or when I'm trying to motivate you. Or cheer you up."

He slid into a kitchen chair and flopped his head on the table. "In that case, I could use the chocolate."

"Uh-oh. What's going on?"

Trevor propped his head up on his hands and told her all about why Molly wasn't talking to him and that he and Libby had made lots of promises to lots of kids. "It's making me skyrocket in the popularity department, but I'm worried Kip won't get to our ideas. He keeps working on other projects . . . random projects."

She tilted her head. "How random are we talking?"

"There's a disco ball in the cafeteria, Mom."

She nodded. "Random."

"But that's not all. Today I was eating lunch in our new

lounge, which isn't even a cafeteria anymore, and I couldn't balance my plate of spaghetti because the seats were so plush and there was an umbrella in my drink, which caused . . . Oh, let's not go into details. My point is, I promised Libby I would be open to change." He dipped his head. "But change isn't something I really do, Mom."

She sat down in the chair next to him. "What are you talking about? You can handle change."

"I can't even handle a new seating assignment."

She laughed. "What about when your dad moved out? That was a big one."

He shrugged. "I guess."

"It was hard at first, but I was amazed how quickly you adapted." She ruffled his hair. "Now you video chat with him every Wednesday, and you see him every other weekend. It's become your new routine, and you seem okay with it."

Trevor did like the routine with his dad. It wasn't until his dad moved out that he started drawing so much. Just as a way of dealing with their separation—instead of talking, he drew. It helped him so much that he couldn't stop drawing and pretty much documented every episode in his life—good or bad—in his drawing notebook.

Thankfully, Mr. Jeffries was always there to give him

drawing tips. He'd gotten a lot better, and that made coping with things a lot easier. "I guess you're right, Mom."

She raised a brow. "You're capable of handling lots of changes."

The phone rang and Ms. Jones answered. He waved his hands around wildly to signal he wasn't available for calls. No doubt, it'd be someone else from school pestering him about a makeover request. But Ms. Jones ignored all the hand flailing and said, "It's for you. And so is this."

Trevor looked up, and next to the phone receiver was a fun-size candy bar. It would certainly make this phone call easier to handle. "Thanks," he mouthed to her. "Hello?"

"I think I figured it out," Libby blurted. "Can you come over?"

"Sure."

"Bring Magic Markers and a ruler. Oh! And I'm almost out of ranch dressing!"

Trevor knew the dressing was to calm her nerves. But she never liked to admit that that's what it was for. She often pretended to enjoy the dressing simply because of a change in weather. "Ranch dressing . . . because of the fog rolling in?"

"You know me too well. Hurry." He could almost hear her smiling.

* * *

When Trevor arrived at Libby's house, he found her drawing circles and lines on a poster.

"Maybe this time if I present all the students' ideas in a pro/con chart or a bar graph or a pie chart, he'll see that it's a good idea. Something visual—it makes for good television. That's what he wants! And then we'll do a separate one for Savannah's idea, maybe even use puffy paint."

"You're going through a lot of effort just to impress Savannah."

"She's never spoken to me before, but now she's acting like I'm this cool, important person. She even waved at me when we were standing in the bus line. At least I *think* it was me—Corey Long was standing right behind me."

Trevor felt a tingle. He'd heard these words before. She went through this the summer that she was friends with Jessica Lymon. Libby was so wrapped up in what Jessica thought of her that she was crushed when Jessica didn't want to be friends anymore. And Trevor worried the same thing was happening now.

"Aren't you sensing a pattern here?"

"Pattern?"

"You know . . . Jessica Lymon . . . now Savannah Maxwell."

Libby looked up at the ceiling and paused as if she were considering this connection. Then: "Nope. Two totally different things."

Trevor sighed. He guessed being the best friend meant you couldn't always stop your friend from getting hurt. But you could try to find a magic washcloth to heal her when she did. Or something close to it. For Libby, it was ranch dressing.

"Here you go." He pulled out a packet from his bag and handed it over.

She gave an embarrassed grin. "Thanks." She dipped some carrots and munched happily. "I know! For our bar graph, let's glue on some ribbon accents—for flair!"

Trevor nodded and held the ribbon in place while she glued it on. "We should show it to him first thing at lunch break. That way we won't miss him," he said.

"And we'll make sure the cameras are rolling."

"Just make sure nothing's in my teeth this time."

"Don't worry, Trev. I've got your back."

He felt warmth in his cheeks. His best friend telling him she'd be there for him made him want to do the same for her.

I can do this, he thought. I'm going to be open to change . . . ridiculously plush lounge seating and all.

WESTSIDE
MIDDLE SCHOOL

MAKEOVER
DAY NINE

CHAPTER FOURTEEN

THEIR IDEA—DESPITE ALL ITS PERFECTION AND PRE-planned sparkling teeth—completely fell apart. Because the next day, when Libby and Trevor walked into the library with decorative bar graphs in hand . . . Kip Lee was nowhere to be found.

"Excuse me. Have you seen Mr. Lee? He's usually in here right now." Libby tapped the shoulder of one of the TV crew members who was busy with a new glass snow-leopard pencil sharpener. His pencil was in the leopard's mouth, and he was sharpening it by cranking the tail.

Trevor stood, arms folded, glaring at the fragile glass sharpener. Not exactly a middle school–friendly piece of art. But he had to admit, it was totally rad. No one could say Kip Lee didn't have good taste.

The crew member set the glass leopard sharpener down on the library checkout counter and called out to Mrs. Shulman, the librarian. "A gift for you!" he said with a big smile. He then turned back to Trevor and Libby, and that smile turned to a scowl. "Kip was called up to the office."

Libby sighed with relief. "Whew. I'm glad everything's okay."

The man wiped his brow. "Oh, I wouldn't say that. He got called in by the vice principal. That Decker guy. And he looked pretty mad."

"I'm sure it's fine," Libby explained. "Our vice principal gets mad a lot. I think he's supposed to."

Mrs. Shulman stepped up to the counter and pulled the pencil sharpener closer to her. "He wasn't mad. He was furious." She used the sleeve of her sweater to buff a smudge off the face of the leopard and whispered, "Gorgeous."

Libby smiled nervously. "Excuse us." She grabbed Trevor by the arm and yanked him out to the hallway so no one else could hear. "Something's going on. We need to get to Decker's office and find out what it is."

Trevor's face went white. He didn't want to be involved in any situation in which a vice principal was furious. "No, we should forget we heard any of this and go back to the cafeteria."

Libby paced back and forth as she spoke. "We'll stroll by Decker's office and get a drink of water from the fountain located diagonally from his door. That way—"

"Let's go get ranch dressing from the salad bar."

"—we can hear everything they're saying, but it looks like we're just really thirsty."

"And some croutons?"

She clamped down on his shoulder. "Trevor. Are you thirsty?"

He winced. "Sort of . . . ?"

Libby leaned in and narrowed her eyes, her football coach stance. "I'll ask you again. Are. You. Thirsty?"

He nodded and gave her the only answer she wanted to hear. "Yes, Coach."

"Let's do this."

They rushed down the hall, around a corner, and up to the water fountain across from Decker's office. His door was slightly open, and they could see that Kip was seated in a chair across from Decker's desk. His legs were crossed, and he looked quite casual, as if he was simply discussing the weather.

Decker, on the other hand, did *not* appear to be making casual weather observations. He paced behind his desk, gripping a piece of paper and reading from it out loud through clenched teeth.

As Vice Principal Decker spoke, Libby and Trevor went about their plan:

Drink.

Eavesdrop.

Repeat.

It worked perfectly; they could hear every word.

"Expenses? What do you mean *expenses*?!" Decker's voice boomed.

"The fine print," Kip said. "Didn't you read the fine print in the contract? It said our TV show is responsible for the cost of the remodel, but since we had to travel here, the school is to pay for all our expenses. Meals, lodging, extra clothing, and I believe there's an 'other' category."

"Oh, no," Libby whispered.

Trevor finished his sip of water and lifted his head. "What?" He wiped his mouth with the back of his hand.

"Decker and I didn't actually read the whole contract."

"Libby! You *always* read things carefully. You read the ingredients on cereal before you eat it—every single time!"

She bit her lip. "I was just so excited. When the contract came in, I read over his shoulder, but I was bouncing on my toes and I kept saying 'flip the page, flip the page!'" Libby shook her head. "Decker was just as excited as I was . . . and he kept flipping the pages. We must have skimmed over the expenses section. I just hope there aren't *too* many expenses listed on there."

Through the crack in the door, they saw Decker jab his finger at the paper. "Dinner for eight at Yamagi sushi restaurant. Dinner for eight at Kokumu sushi restaurant. Dinner for eight at Roshuki sushi restaurant. Dinner for eight at Olive Garden. Can you explain all this?!"

"You can only eat so much sushi. And those bread sticks are delicious," Kip said.

Decker rubbed his forehead and continued. "Ten hotel rooms. Why ten rooms?"

"Some of my staff brought their puppies."

"Thirty-two large lattes, daily deliveries of kale-and-beet smoothies—"

"Look, most schools just have bake sales and potlucks to feed us," Kip explained. "They offer to have us stay in their homes because they don't have the money. So I was pretty impressed when Libby handed me that list of places to eat and shop."

There was a gasp out in the hall. That was followed by the sound of someone stomping on someone's toe. And *that* sound was followed by someone yelling, "Ouch, Trevor!"

Decker peeked out his office door. "Trevor. Libby. Come in here."

Libby started to head inside, but Trevor hesitated. She reached out and pulled on his arm. "Come with me."

"But I didn't do anything wrong."

She glared at him. "I need you."

"Why?"

She clamped down on his arm tighter. "You need to pick me up when I faint from guilt."

He couldn't argue with that.

They both scuffled into Decker's office and stuck close to the far wall, as if their backs were magnetized to it.

"I'm guessing you overheard this conversation?" Decker folded his arms.

Libby nodded and looked down at her feet.

Decker's voice then softened, as if he'd just been defeated in the final seconds of the Super Bowl. Or a really competitive spelling bee. "Then let me go down the rest of the list. Size twelve Italian leather sandals. Four silk hand-monogrammed towels." He peeked at Kip over the paper, his forehead now covered in sweat beads.

"I need my name on my towels, otherwise I get confused," Kip explained. "And I needed new open-toed shoes. That blacktop out there all but ruined my first pair."

Decker cleared his throat and kept reading. "New replacement filters for the floor buffer. And a glass snow leopard pencil sharpener." He carefully laid the paper down on his desk and sat down slowly, making an attempt to remain calm. "Can you tell me *why* you bought floor buffer filters and a leopard?"

"They're for Wilson and Mrs. Shulman. I had to keep your staff happy during the remodel." Kip leaned forward and pointed to the bottom of the page. "I believe that falls under the 'other' category."

Decker rubbed his temples. "These expenses total up to *thousands* of dollars."

This is unbelievable, Libby thought. Maybe he added wrong. Surely he didn't just say *thousands*.

He did. And no matter how much Libby hoped this was all a large mathematical error, the fact that the school now owed Kip Lee thousands of dollars was not going away. This was all very, very real. What could she do? Hold a bake sale?!

Golden Nugget Cookies: $475 each

100% Pure Velvet Cupcakes: $975 each

Diamond Encrusted Cakes:
$5,000 + $5,000 for emerald sprinkled frosting

This might not work. HOLA! Kitty Cat!

Kip stood up and tugged on his shirt to flatten out any wrinkles. "If it's any consolation, my crew and I have been having a great stay. This town is lovely—sort of. Anyway, we'll be done with the renovation by Friday. I'll need a check for these expenses, plus expenses for the rest of the week, on Friday. Producer's orders." Kip walked out of the room, whistling a tune with his chin held high.

Decker sat back in his chair. He took in a long breath and let it out. And then he did it again. After what felt like three weeks, he finally spoke. "This is my fault. I can't believe I rushed through the contract and didn't read it carefully."

Libby stepped forward, tears stinging her eyes. "It's my fault, too. I was bouncing so much—I'm sure I distracted you."

He held his hand up. "I accept the blame. Now I have to figure out how to pay for all this."

"Mr. Decker, I . . . I'm so sorry. Maybe we could—"

He pointed at his door and lowered his head. "Just go on back to lunch, kids."

As Trevor and Libby left, they immediately heard the slow click of the office door closing shut behind them. And though she hadn't fainted, the guilt weighed heavily on Libby. She couldn't hold back the tears.

Trevor Jones

Shocked.
Totally.

12:54 p.m.

I never saw this coming. Libby Gardner . . . did NOT read the fine print. What?!

And I knew ALL ALONG that Kip Lee was trouble. Or part of the time. Okay, right at the beginning, I didn't like the guy. But still, that probably means I'm a good judge of character.

But there's no way I'd say "I told you so" to Libby. Knowing her, this will turn her into a wreck. I'm proud of her for not fainting, though. Or going numb.

And my guess is she'll come up with a way to fix this. Or call me to come up with a way to fix this.

I'd better get busy on a list.

Libby Gardner

Holding back tears,
unsuccessfully

12:55 p.m.

I'm not going to cry. Not anymore. I'm going to find the right words and the perfect way to say them and get Kip to forget this whole expenses thing. It was simply a misunderstanding. People skip over the fine print all the time. Probably.

Even though I usually read the fine print—sometimes twice. I'm probably the only person who actually reads through the terms of agreement when there are updates on my phone. When I click, "Yes, I've read these terms and agree," it's ACTUALLY TRUE.

So I really can't explain why I didn't do it this time.

[fidgets with the hem on her skirt]

And what is Savannah Maxwell going to think when she hears about this? She's everything I want to be in a class president—a good leader, likable, and fashion forward. Sometimes I wonder if I'm ANY of those things.

155

But if I'm going to prove I AM a good leader, I have to fix this. I'm not even going to ask Trevor for help this time. The guy's done enough for me already. He's moved furniture, painted walls, made an exception to his "no changes" life motto . . . He's the best. But maybe it's time for me to stop leaning on him so much.

I was the one who got us into this mess, and I'll find a way out.

CHAPTER FIFTEEN

DESPITE THE FACT THAT VICE PRINCIPAL DECKER SAID he'd figure out how to solve this, Libby Gardner was not the type to stand by and do nothing. It was time for a one-on-one talk with Kip Lee.

After school ended, Libby rushed out to the blacktop. But heading in her direction was Savannah Maxwell, with a determined look on her face. An eighth-grade-class-president look.

Savannah stormed up to Libby, her boots making a clicking sound on the blacktop. "I tried to talk to Kip, but it didn't work. This new outfit didn't help one bit. He said he can't put in my mirrors because there's not enough money now. Apparently the school owes him for expenses."

She stuck her hand on her hip and shifted her weight—the angry eighth-grade-class-president stance. "Would you mind explaining that?"

Libby knew that telling her the truth would probably ruin her chances of a friendship with Savannah. But lying wasn't something Libby Gardner did. She stood up tall and said, "I didn't read the fine print on the contract."

"What? A class president *always* reads the fine print on a contract. Or a *good* president would."

Wow, Libby thought. Rude much?

"Look, it's true we should have read it. It was just too exciting, and we skipped it. But you have to trust me—I'm going to talk to Kip right now and fix this."

"Trust? You didn't include me in the first place. And now your project is starting to fall apart." She crossed her arms and raised a brow. "Not a single thing I've planned as president has been anything but perfect. It's looking like your chances of becoming eighth grade class president are zero-point-zero." She stormed off, the sound of her heels clicking on the blacktop fading with every step.

Libby spun around to face Kip's trailer, ready to do whatever it took to solve this problem. She wasn't about to let this ruin her chances for next year's presidency.

Stepping up to Kip's trailer door, she wasn't quite sure

what she was about to say. Should she be sweet? Angry? Sickly?

As long as she was assertive enough, she figured he'd have to listen. A direct heart-to-heart conversation, that's all she needed.

She knocked without hesitation.

And she knocked again.

Loud sounds were coming from inside.

Another knock.

Finally, Kip opened his door. And she was shocked to find that this wasn't going to be a one-on-one discussion at all. His trailer was completely crammed with students.

Some kids were playing video games, a few were watching TV on a jumbo flat screen, three kids were raiding his fridge for snacks, and Corey Long was playing darts along with half of the Westside baseball team. It was chaos. Total, complete chaos!

But she had to admit, this was the swankiest trailer she'd ever seen. Even the uplighting along the ceiling changed colors, like in a dance club. She wasn't sure whether to be disgusted or amazed.

"Come on in, Libby. I'm in the middle of an epic dartboard game!" Kip's voice trailed off as he retreated inside.

Squeezing into the trailer, Libby made her way through

the thick stew of students, trying to get to Kip. But before she could get over to the dartboard, she heard someone call her name. "Libby! Hi!"

Cindy Applegate had bounced up next to her, holding a bowl of ice cream. "It's nonfat pomegranate sorbet. Exactly what Kip asked for," Cindy said in a loud voice to be heard over the crowd. "Wanna come with me to give it to him?"

Hardly, Libby thought. She didn't want to stand around giving Kip strange ice cream that sounded expensive. She was done playing games. They had a serious problem, and it needed to be solved. *Now.*

"Cindy, I actually need everyone out of here."

"What? I can't hear you!"

Libby knew being class president usually meant being in charge of events and fund-raisers. But being in charge also meant that in this moment—as much as she disliked it—she was going to have to raise her voice.

"Everyone get QUIET!"

No one had ever heard this octave of Libby Gardner's voice. She'd always had such a soft touch. Not anymore.

The cramped trailer immediately silenced. One could even hear the click of the TV being turned off.

All eyes turned to Libby as she cleared her throat. "Thank you. Now, we have some business to deal with, and

I need to speak with Mr. Lee. Everyone please wait outside."

They grumbled, but they could sense the seriousness in Libby's voice, so they all willingly exited the trailer.

All but one, that is.

Libby pointed at the door. "You too, Cindy."

"But . . . but I love business! I'm really good at it!"

As the trailer emptied out, Libby realized she'd probably need a witness if she got Kip to agree to drop the expenses. She'd seen enough nighttime TV to know that.

"Fine. Cindy, you can stay." She turned to Kip. "Can we all sit down?"

"Sure." Kip grabbed a spoon and started in on the bowl of sorbet.

The three scooted around a small table built into the trailer wall. The benches they were sitting on were covered in a purple satin, one of her favorite colors and one of her favorite materials. But this was no time for design talk. It was time for business.

Libby folded her hands on top of the table. "I realize we owe you quite a bit for all these expenses. But this was all just a misunderstanding." She pressed her lips together. That was *not* the word she meant to use! *You can do this, Lib.* "Okay, so it wasn't a *misunderstanding* exactly . . . more like an oversight. That contract had so many words—

some extremely small—and I was simply in a rush to get the makeover started so we could benefit from your incredible knowledge." Surely flattery would get her somewhere.

Kip nodded in agreement and scooped up another spoonful of pomegranate sorbet. It was working.

Libby's knees bounced under the table with excitement. "You're nodding in agreement. So does that mean we can just forget about charging the school for all these expenses?"

Cindy smiled and gave her a "way-to-go" raised eyebrow look.

This is going really well, Libby thought. And Cindy's witnessing it! Thank goodness for nighttime TV.

He set his spoon down and dabbed at each side of his mouth with a napkin. "There's no way around it—the contract is binding. I'm sorry, but the expenses are due on Friday."

"But Friday is only three days away!" Libby shrieked.

He stood up and walked over to his marble sink to rinse off his spoon. "You're the creative one. You keep coming up with these design ideas. I'm sure you can think of a quick fund-raiser."

"A *quick* fund-raiser?" Libby bit at her lip. "My highest-grossing fund-raiser was from fifth grade, and it was a bake sale during a car wash where we sold raffle tickets for a three-night beach vacation. Even then, we only raised $364—which was a school record!" She dropped her head in her hands. "But that took me *weeks* to plan. There's no way I can raise thousands of dollars by Friday."

"Don't worry. You and Decker will figure it out." Kip then started scrolling on his phone.

Libby glanced over at Cindy. She'd said she was good at business. Did she have *any* ideas? "Help?" Libby mouthed to her.

But Cindy was more comfortable in business matters that involved fund-raisers her mother was organizing. So as hard as it was for Cindy to admit, this was out of her league. The look Libby was giving her, though, was downright pitiful.

Out of the blue, Cindy felt a new sensation: helpfulness. Surely she could think of a way to get Libby out of this mess. But getting Kip to change his mind was looking impossible, no matter how many lattes she brought.

Libby waited for Cindy to give her an answer, a suggestion—anything. But all she did was give a helpless little shrug. So much for Cindy being good at business. This meeting was over.

Libby pushed her hands off the table, jumped up, and

flew out the trailer door without saying another word. She wished she'd never asked Cindy to stay back with her; now she'd seen her in a weak moment, and Cindy would probably use it against her in some way.

Libby ran across the blacktop, a light mist hitting her face. She needed her space, time to breathe, a place to think—

"Wait up!" Cindy ran up behind her.

"What do you want, Cindy?" Libby threw her hands up and faced her. "I have other things to worry about, and I don't have time for you to be rude to me."

"I ran out here to tell you I'm sorry. I actually wanted to help you back there, but I couldn't think of anything."

Libby tilted her head. "You wanted to *help*?"

"Yes! Come on, let's go figure this out." She grabbed Libby by the arm and pulled her toward the parking lot. "This mist is horrible for my hair. Plus you missed your bus, so my mom will take you home."

Libby breathed a sigh of relief. "Thanks." She couldn't believe she was getting help from Cindy Applegate. This might be exactly what she needed.

The two of them would talk the entire way home and figure this problem out.

For sure.

Cindy Applegate

Leaning against her
mom's SUV

3:15 p.m.

What? No, no, we didn't figure it out. Are you
kidding me? I mean, did you do the MATH? It's
THOUSANDS of dollars in THREE days. That's simple
addition, if you repeat it, which is actually multiplication. Or whatever. What I'm trying to say
is this: even Betty Crocker herself couldn't hold
a bake sale and raise that much money.

But Libby and I did chat all the way home.
Apparently we BOTH love the color periwinkle, and
we BOTH think Saturday is the best day of the
week, and we BOTH can't stand chocolate that has
nuts in it—it's such a waste of good chocolate!
Nuts belong in jars or smooshed into peanut butter, and that's IT! And Libby agrees with me, so
we're going to see if there are some petitions
online we could sign about this nuts-in-chocolate
issue.

But that's AFTER we solve this pay-thousands-of-dollars-by-Friday problem. Which, as it turns out, is a REALLY hard math problem. Maybe our hardest. And that doesn't even take into account the fact that we'd have to COUNT all that money. That's even MORE math.

Gosh, including our upcoming science test, this is SUCH a busy week.

I need an assistant.

WESTSIDE
MIDDLE SCHOOL

MAKEOVER
DAY ELEVEN

CHAPTER SIXTEEN

LIBBY AND CINDY HAD SPENT ALL DAY WEDNESDAY brainstorming ways to earn money.

But no luck.

Libby had even called Trevor on the phone that night (three or five times) to talk about ideas. They stayed up late—*very* late. That explained why Trevor arrived at school on Thursday barely awake.

It was art class, and Trevor had fallen asleep.

Mr. Jeffries tapped on his desk. "You're drooling on your paper."

Not his best moment.

Trevor attempted to sit up straight. *Attempted.* "Sorry for falling asleep. I stayed up too late last night." He wavered in his seat like a palm tree on a windy day.

Jones Family

Ways to Earn Money for Kip's Expenses:

1. Bake sale: buy one chocolate chip cookie, receive one free day of housecleaning (we don't clean microwaves. Gross.)

2. Bake sale idea amended: just chocolate chip cookies.

3. Make puppets, put on a play, and sell the puppets at the play. And other merchandising! Puppet stickers to go on key chains, coffee mugs, backpacks, and detention slips.

4. Write a screenplay about a depressed puppet. Sell the rights.

5. Sell the school.

FOUND NEXT TO TREVOR'S BED

Mr. Jeffries sat down next to him and clamped down on his shoulder for a moment until he was sitting upright and still. "Want to tell me what's going on, Trevor?"

"Last night I was trying to solve a problem." Yawn. "We're trying to figure out how to make money to cover

Kip Lee's expenses. I made a list, but I never came up with the answer."

Mr. Jeffries rolled his eyes. "The school has to pay for expenses?"

"He ate a lot of sushi."

Mr. Jeffries took a deep breath and reached over to the cabinet behind Trevor, pulling out a piece of blank white paper—drool-free—and a box of markers. "Try to draw your way out of the problem. Using the other side of your brain can help."

Without hesitation, Trevor started sketching ideas. Mr. Jeffries's suggestion was impressive—draw *and* solve problems. Multitasking at its finest.

Trevor drew asteroids and lasers and an alien revolution. Creative, yes, but not very practical. By his fourth drawing, he finally came up with a possible solution. One that didn't involve outer space. (Though that would have been totally cool.)

It was such a simple idea, he wasn't sure it would work. But it had a better chance than something involving outer space.

When he got to lunch, Trevor sat next to Libby and slyly slid his drawing across the table to her. "Here it is," he said. "My new idea."

She unfolded the paper and looked it over.

Better than my alien revolution idea

FOUND IN TREVOR'S NOTEBOOK

Libby flicked her eyes up. "You think we should beg?"

"It may be our only hope. Unless you came up with something better?"

Libby had to admit to herself that she had spent her whole ride home with Cindy on Tuesday talking about nuts and their favorite shade of purple. Then on Wednesday, they talked more about a No Chocolate With Nuts petition than about the Kip Lee expense dilemma. And while it had been almost—dare she say—*enjoyable* chatting with Cindy, she hadn't come up with any new ideas to solve the problem.

When she'd spoken with Kip in his trailer, she'd taken a business approach. Lacking emotion. And it didn't work. So maybe Trevor's simple idea was the way to go. Show *feelings*.

It was time to beg.

Libby nodded. "Time to get on our puppy-dog looks."

During their lunch break, Trevor and Libby tracked down Kip in the front lobby. He was placing rocks in a meditation fountain.

"Mr. Lee, can we speak with you?" Libby asked.

It was good timing, since the rest of the students were still busy eating. She figured they could boldly beg without public embarrassment.

"There you guys are!" Corey Long yelled from the *other* side of the meditation fountain. They hadn't even noticed him.

So much for public embarrassment being left out of the equation.

Corey was organizing pebbles, and his hair had flopped over, looking exhausted. Trevor didn't know hair could look so overwhelmed.

"I've been doing work . . . by . . . *myself*," Corey said.

"Gee, the horror," Trevor said under his breath because he really didn't want to say it *over* his breath. He was not in the mood for a hallway-tripping incident.

"What do you need to talk about?" Kip stepped back to admire his rock placement.

Trevor tugged on Libby's elbow as he said to Kip, "Actually, we could talk to you about it later." The last thing he wanted to do was be involved in a moment of begging while in Corey's presence.

Trevor quickly whispered in Libby's ear. "Not now. Not in front of Corey."

Kip crossed his arms. "I have time right now. Go ahead and ask. I may be too busy later—that janitor's closet isn't going to demolish itself."

Libby whispered back to Trevor, "We have to do it now. Who cares if it's in front of Corey? Stop worrying about him."

"But he's always trying to humiliate me. Do I have to make it so easy for him?"

Kip's eyes zinged back and forth between the two as

they bickered. "Are you two lovebirds done whispering? Let's get on with it."

"Lovebirds?" Trevor threw his arms in the air like he was innocent. "Whoa. We're not—"

"Us?! No." Libby's cheeks turned bubblegum pink.

"We're aren't—"

"No way—"

"We're just—"

"Best friends," they answered in unison.

Then Trevor and Libby both turned and stared off in opposite directions, allowing for a moment of silence— thick and weird. Like Canadian bacon.

Taking a deep breath, Kip finally broke the silence. "I don't have much time. Just ask your question."

"Let's kneel," Libby said as she pulled on Trevor and got down on her knees.

"Me? I thought only *you* really needed to be kneeling."

"That's how you drew it in the picture! We were begging side by side!"

"That was symbolism!"

"Not this again." Kip rolled his eyes. "Enough with the banter. You're both brilliant. Someone, please, just ask me a question!"

Libby yanked Trevor down next to her—as symbolically depicted in his drawing—and said in a sweet voice, "Please, Mr. Lee. I had no idea how the expenses were handled because I did not read the fine print. I'm truly sorry. It's just that I was so excited we had won, and I made a mistake. This is all my fault." Libby's lower lip quivered, hopefully for added emotional impact.

As Trevor attempted to listen to Libby's heartfelt-ishness, all he could hear was Corey's laughter as he stood over Kip's shoulder. Obviously this would somehow be used against him in the near future. His reputation at Westside would be obliterated, yet again.

Awesome.

But then came a girl's voice. "Whatcha doing, Libby?"

Not wanting to look, Libby closed her eyes tight and elbowed Trevor. "Please tell me that's not her."

He turned and peeked. "Yep. It's Savannah Maxwell."

"I know I asked for a favor, but no need to beg, girl!" Savannah called out.

Libby clenched her jaw and slowly turned around to face her. She hesitantly waved. "Ha. Sure thing . . . girl."

Did I just use the word girl? *I hate that word!*

"Savannah, wait up," Corey yelled out. "I have lots to tell you." He sauntered over to her, and the two oozed down the hall like the king and queen of their own country called Perfection.

Libby turned back and glared at Trevor. "So. Embarrassing. Why didn't we just do one of your other suggestions?"

He shrugged. "Not enough lasers."

Kip laughed and grabbed Libby and Trevor by the hands and pulled them up to their feet. "You two can stop worrying. Didn't Decker tell you? The expenses have all been taken care of."

Trevor and Libby looked at each other in disbelief. Did he just say what they thought he said? The expenses are *paid for*?

Trevor tilted his head. "What do you mean?"

"There was a school board meeting last night. They added Decker on as a last-minute agenda item to their budget discussion. They talked it through, and the board figured out a plan to get the expenses paid for. We can even add those items you requested. We're already working on those mirrors in the girls' bathroom." Kip looked at Trevor. "And those rugs you asked for, Tom."

Trevor was so stunned he didn't even attempt to correct Kip. "O—okay. And what about our other suggestions?"

Kip pulled out a piece of paper from his pocket and read from his list. "The extra bacon bits, a volleyball court, weight room . . . yep. All of it. We'll get it done."

Libby clasped her hands together. "This is amazing news! Oh my gosh, thank you." She twirled right there in her spot, and when she finally came to a stop, she faced Trevor, slightly off balance. "I'm soooo relieved. Let's go tell Savannah the good news! Whoa, everything's spinning."

Trevor followed her to keep her from tipping over. But he didn't feel relieved. Not yet. He'd remembered Wilson telling him how hard he had fought to get the board to approve the replacement filters for his floor buffer, but there wasn't enough money in the budget. So how did Decker get this money so easily?

An uneasy feeling came over Trevor. Something about this situation stunk like a week-old tuna sandwich.

Corey Long

Sharing his
feelings—not
typical

1:02 p.m.

That begging thing that just happened back there?
HYSTERICAL. I would NEVER get on a knee and beg
someone. Too many people have phones, and too many
phones have cameras. Not worth it

That's what I was explaining to Savannah when
I walked her down the hall. All about my fear of
cameras because the pictures could end up being
passed around and how you might get made fun of
because you wore sweater vests and bow ties every
day in fifth grade.

**[clears throat; glances around to make sure no
on else can hear]**

Uh, yeah, see I went through a severe vest/
bow tie phase a few years ago. I thought I looked
pretty good, but the other kids were BRUTAL. So
I snapped out of it, and after a few sessions
with a life coach, I learned to only focus on my
STRENGTHS. I'm sure she meant my hair.

Anyway, like I said, I was explaining all this

181

to Savannah, but she could hardly hear me over the sound of her boots clacking on the linoleum. Where did she get those weapons?

ANOTHER reason I walked away with Savannah— other than to explain my deep thoughts on stuff— was because I really don't want to help that Kip Lee guy out anymore. Right now I'm totally focused on my comic book–writing career. Luckily I found my missing comic book. . . . It was outside the janitor's closet in a box labeled Things That Will Catch Fire When Lit with a Match.

I'm glad I found it, bro. NO ONE can find out I drew it.

But eventually I might tell Libby—she'd probably like that I'm an accomplished writer and illustrator. Except I'm not going to tell her yet.

I want her to like me for more than just my mind.

Wilson

Near his demolished
Supply Containment
Unit, not pleased

1:04 p.m.

This day is what you'd call A DISASTER. They still haven't organized my Supply Containment Unit so that I can actually FIND THINGS.

And to make matters worse, I was reading this comic book I found in the boys' bathroom. I'm not sure who wrote it, but it is EPIC.

I had just gotten to the part where the janitor's floor buffer turns into a Transformer and attempts to take over the vice principal's office. But now the comic book is missing! I HAVE to find out what happens next.

I will find that book.

Mark my words.

CHAPTER SEVENTEEN

As Libby headed down the hallway, practically dragging Trevor behind her, they noticed Vice Principal Decker coming out of Mr. Jeffries's art classroom. When they got near, they noticed a strange thing. Mr. Jeffries followed Decker out to the hall, and both had blank looks on their faces. Sad looks. Vacation-canceled looks. A-kitten-has-been-poisoned looks.

But strangely enough, that wasn't even the strange part.

Decker and Mr. Jeffries saw Trevor and Libby walking up to them, but neither said a word. They just stood there in the hall—blinking, staring. There was severe awkwardness hanging in the air.

One would think this would be the moment for Decker

to explain to Libby and Trevor exactly how/where/when/ why the expenses had been paid for. One would think he would console Libby and let her know that everything was taken care of and there was no need to worry any longer. One would think he would say . . . something.

But none of that happened.

Instead, Decker sighed, stuffed his hands in the pockets of his linen pants, and walked away in silence.

Trevor and Libby looked at each other, mouths gaping, as if they were both having the same thought:

Why didn't Decker mention the expenses getting paid? Isn't this weird? And isn't it weirder that we're just staring at each other, not actually saying any of this out loud?

Mr. Jeffries quietly retreated back into his room, and Libby and Trevor followed him. Surely he knew something.

The art room was quiet and empty, with the only light coming from the window overlooking the amazing scenery of the teacher parking lot. Mr. Jeffries walked straight over to the window and looked out past his Toyota, as if he was deep in thought.

"That was strange back there with Vice Principal Decker," Trevor blurted. "Do you know what that was all about?"

Without turning around to look at them, Mr. Jeffries

said in a low voice, "It was about the school remodel. Vice Principal Decker went to the school board meeting last night and spoke during their budget talk. A talk that was also supposed to involve the approval of my art supplies for the rest of the year. But the cost of my supplies came out to be about the same as what is owed to Kip Lee."

Libby swallowed hard. She was worried where this was going. "So . . . they . . . What are you saying?"

He turned around and leaned back against the counter. "They voted to suspend art class for the year in order to pay off the expenses. I'm going to be teaching a math club instead. Worksheets are cheap. And they said if we put an exclamation mark in the club name, kids will think it's fun. I'm told they even used the phrase *win-win*."

"No, it's not! It's a lose-lose." There was panic in Trevor's voice. "That's not the answer. You have to tell them no. You can't suspend art class! Right, Libby? We have to tell Decker to figure out a different way to get the money!"

Trevor looked over at Libby, hoping she'd reassure Mr. Jeffries, but she was nervously twirling her hair, not giving either of them eye contact. "I . . . hmm . . ." she said to the wall.

"Hang on a second, Mr. J. We'll be right back." Trevor dragged Libby out to the hall.

"We *are* going to talk to Decker, right?"

She winced. "I don't know what to say, Trev. I mean, it *does* solve our problem."

"*Our* problem? *You're* the one who got the school into this mess. And now you're willing to let art class get canceled just so the school can be redecorated?"

"I'm doing this because, if you hadn't noticed, everyone has been excited. Excited about their school! *That's* what this is all about. It's not easy being the class president. It's not easy to make everyone happy. I'm just trying to make the right decisions."

"The school needs an art class, not beanbags and palm trees." Trevor whipped around and stormed off.

"Where are you going?"

"I'm going to talk to Decker," he yelled back, still walking away. "And you can find another partner for your design team. I quit."

Trevor Jones

Pacing the hall,
pretty ticked

1:42 p.m.

I'm sure Libby isn't talking to me now. Whatever. But if anyone's keeping score, that's two friends not speaking to me—Libby AND Molly. And I'll probably be up to three once Marty finds out I'm not going to be helping out with getting those rugs he wanted.

But maybe—just MAYBE—if I can convince Decker to keep Art, I could start drawing at lunch again. And it's entirely possible Molly will think I'm some sort of hero for saving art class since it's her favorite. And that will be enough.

So I have to hurry and go find the vice principal so we can have a heart-to-heart chat.

[scratches his head]

That is a sentence I never thought I'd say.

CHAPTER EIGHTEEN

IT DIDN'T TAKE **T**REVOR LONG. **H**E FOUND **D**ECKER drinking from the water fountain outside his office. When he stood up, their eyes locked. Trevor knew this was his moment—he'd do whatever it took to change Decker's mind. Negotiation. Compromise. His mom's famous chili. Whatever it took.

Trevor rushed up to him. "I heard about the decision to suspend art class. Isn't there another way we can handle this? Like maybe—"

Decker held his hand up. "I wish there was another solution, Trevor. But I had to make a quick decision, and there weren't any other options, to be quite honest."

"But art class is awesome. We need to use the other side of our brains. And sometimes people need art to cope." He blushed at this admission. "I mean, that's what I *hear*."

The emotional-cover-up maneuver. He knew it well.

"Trevor, the decision has been made."

"Chili. You just need my mom's chili and then we can talk some more—"

Decker smirked. He appreciated the effort Trevor was making, and he didn't like having to make a hard decision like this—especially when Ms. Jones's chili was involved.

This making-tough-decisions wasn't the part of the job he liked. He liked making sure students were following correct dress-code regulations—that was so black and white. But this? Not so easy. No win-win, though one of the school board members had used that phrase. Decker didn't agree, but he couldn't come up with a better solution.

He patted Trevor on the shoulder. "I'm sorry. Truly." Then he turned and headed down the hall in search of dress-code violators to perk up his mood.

Trevor turned around to head back to class. But that's when he ran smack-dab into Molly. "What was *that* about?" she asked.

Molly hadn't spoken to him in days, but suddenly she'd appeared, collided with him, and was now asking him a question. Progress! But this wasn't any ordinary question. He was going to have to tell her that her father just suspended art class. The one class she truly loved. And all because Libby and Decker didn't read the fine print.

Molly tapped her foot, waiting for his answer. "Well?" she said. "Why was he apologizing to you? I don't think I've *ever* heard Dad say he was sorry." Other than the time he apologized for eating the last stick of Molly's black licorice, it was really true. He never used the words *I'm sorry* in Molly's presence. So she wondered why Trevor was so lucky.

He started from the beginning, from Kip Lee buying size twelve Italian leather sandals, all the way up to Mr. Jeffries now teaching the Multiplication Club! instead of art class. "But hey, you and I are talking now, so that's a good thing, right?" Trevor smiled weakly, hoping she'd see this tiny silver lining.

Molly didn't notice any brightness. "This is bad," she said. Molly's dad had been transferred to several different middle schools already, and a situation like this screamed transfer. Molly couldn't handle one more move—she was ready to stay put. Which meant she needed to do something quick. "It's all bad, Trevor. I gotta go." She slipped into the chaos of the hallway and was gone.

Bad? Trevor thought. Which part was the bad part? The being-on-speaking-terms part? Or the no-more-Art part? This was so confusing.

* * *

Trevor stepped inside the art room, dismayed there were already empty cardboard boxes strewn about. Mr. Jeffries was pulling down art projects from the bulletin board when he noticed Trevor enter the room. He pulled out a thumbtack from between his teeth and looked up at him.

Trevor didn't wait for formal greetings. "Why can't they get rid of P.E.? Kickballs are expensive, and those things are dangerous. No one ever got pegged in the face by dried macaroni."

"That's not true." Corey Long had walked in. "I've totally pegged someone with macaroni. But it was cooked, not dried—that probably would have been a better way to go."

Is Corey everywhere? Trevor wondered. And who throws cooked macaroni without thinking through it first? It's pretty obvious.

"Here you go, Corey." Mr. Jeffries grabbed a stack of books and handed them over.

"Thanks, Mr. J. This isn't fair."

As Corey walked out, Trevor quickly took a closer look and noticed the stack of books were *drawing books*. So Trevor and Molly *weren't* the only ones—Corey loved Art, too? Interesting.

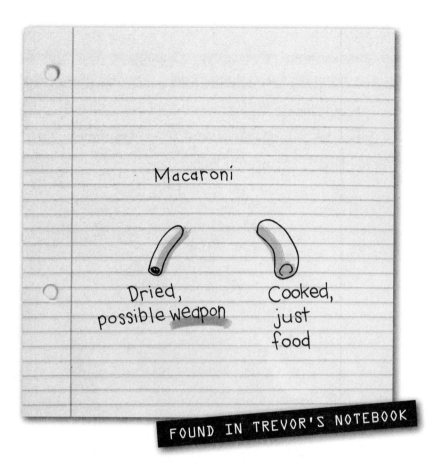

Macaroni

Dried,
possible weapon

Cooked,
just
food

FOUND IN TREVOR'S NOTEBOOK

Looking around the room, Trevor noticed the blank paper was still on the shelf. He tried to make one last-ditch effort.

"We could draw. We should use the other side of our brains to find an answer, just like you told me before, Mr. J."

But Mr. Jeffries gave a halfhearted shrug and sunk into his squeaky chair. "I can't, Trevor. I have to look over this contract and get it back to Mr. Decker. It's too late.

I appreciate you trying to help; I really do." He looked around the room, letting out a long exhale. "Will you help me pack up this stuff?"

Trevor sighed, realizing Mr. Jeffries was right. . . . It was too late. "Of course I'll help."

Trevor Jones

Very perplexed

2:21 p.m.

So Molly and I aren't talking. Libby and I aren't talking. And Vice Principal Decker just APOLOGIZED to me.

Nope. I have NO IDEA what's going on.

But we have beanbags and soft lighting, and Corey Long likes Art.

It's sorta like my life is one of those snow globes and someone just shook it up, and everything is all blurry and chaotic and you can't see anything, and you wonder if the miniature people living inside the tiny buildings will even SURVIVE.

CHAPTER NINETEEN

IT IS ONLY A RUMOR THAT TEACHERS AND VICE PRINCIPALS live 24/7 inside school walls. Research has proven that they do—in fact—have personal lives. In fact, they enjoy all the same things as regular humans: sleep, a good dinner, and some reality TV. Then on the weekend there's yard work and watching movies.

They're pretty regular people.

Usually.

That evening, Vice Principal Decker went home and relaxed on his sofa, trying to block out the horrible day he'd had at school. That disappointed look on Mr. Jeffries's face. All those tough decisions. And having to apologize to that Trevor kid.

Also: the lunch was chicken nuggets *again*? He made a

mental note to start bringing his own lunch. At least he'd requested real fruit be used in the slushee machine Kip had put in the cafeteria. Decker worried a lack of vitamin C in students would result in scurvy and bad decisions about following the dress code. Except that would give him more dress-code violators to spot. So fun.

But today had been filled with all the not-so-fun stuff, and he was ready to kick back and forget.

Comfort: that was his first order of business. He changed into his favorite San Diego Chargers jersey, fleece sweatpants, and fuzzy ladybug slippers. The slippers had been a Christmas gift from Molly, ones she'd given to him ironically—her dad was a tough, serious man, and she wanted to see how he'd react to such a gift.

Surprisingly, he loved them. They were warm and comfortable, plus they were a gift from his daughter. So every night, without fail, he came home from school and slipped them on. At first Molly couldn't believe it, but after a while it became so normal she couldn't imagine him wearing anything else on his feet.

As Decker rested comfortably on the sofa with his ladybug feet propped up, he decided he'd do something unusual: order takeout pizza instead of cooking his regularly scheduled Thursday chicken chow mein. He simply

didn't have the energy. And his wife, the Honorable Mrs. Decker, was still in court and wouldn't be home until late. Mrs. Decker was a judge for the Westside County superior court and often wasn't home because cases needed to be settled. And not by dinnertime.

This left Vice Principal Decker in charge of cooking dinner for Molly, checking that she got her homework done, and making sure she was a happy and well-balanced child.

But Molly was neither happy nor well-balanced.

She didn't play sports. She didn't play instruments.

And she was pretty bummed out on a regular basis.

The one thing that *did* make her happy was drawing pictures. Usually upstairs in her room away from her father, who was always busy cooking some gourmet meal he'd learned online from GourmetDads.com.

So she was shocked when she heard her father yell up the stairs, "The pizza's here. Come on down!"

A pizza? Molly couldn't remember the last time they'd ordered one. She could come up with only one explanation: he must have found out that Art was her favorite class, so he ordered a pizza to make it up to her.

Molly had to admit, she liked the idea of being apologized to through delicious food. She bounded down the stairs, which was highly uncharacteristic for her. Slinking? Yes. Scuffling? Sure. But apologies from her dad were rare, so this called for bounding.

When she peeked around the corner, she saw her dad lounging on the sofa eating a slice, not off their regular dinner plates, but *off his hand*. And the pizza box was carelessly tossed on the coffee table next to a bottle of soda.

Whoa. This might just be the best day of her life.

"Thanks for the pizza, Dad. And the soda and lack of dinner plates. This is nice—really nice."

She shoved her hands in her pockets and waited

for him to start talking. To start apologizing.

But he didn't—he just chewed his food and flipped channels.

Molly decided to take the reins and make this happen. "Was there something you wanted to tell me?"

He reached for another slice. "I love this show. It's *America's Next Top Oil Rig Foreman*. Fascinating!" He talked in between bites and patted the spot next to him. "Sit down and have some pizza with me."

She grabbed a slice and flopped down on the couch. This must be how it was going to go down. Him apologizing while pretending to watch a show. Since her dad knew giving direct eye contact was not her favorite activity, this would make it easier on both of them.

"Why are we eating pizza, Dad?" Molly wanted to plow through the strangeness of the moment and quickly get to the words she wanted to hear.

Mr. Decker said words. But they weren't the ones she was hoping for. "This is the part where Walt tells Jimbo he has a bad attitude," he said. "Want me to rewind it to the beginning?"

She'd had enough. Her attitude was heading south, just like Jimbo's. "Aren't you going to apologize to me?" she blurted.

He sat up straight, startled by her tone. "Apologize? For what?"

"Isn't that why you got this pizza and soda? To butter me up for the apology you're about to lay on me."

"I got the pizza because I had a hard day. I just want to relax." He clicked the TV off and put his ladybug feet on the ground so he could face her. He had the distinct feeling that he needed to give Molly his full attention— eye contact and all. "What am I supposed to apologize for?"

She looked down at her feet, one of her toes sticking out of her worn rainbow tights. And as she stared, it hit her: This whole thing—the soda and delicious food—had nothing to do with her. He had no idea he was supposed to be saying he was sorry.

Her first instinct was to run up to her room. Slam the door. Kick something stuffed. But she was tired of stomping around all the time. Plus she didn't have on boots to make the stomping effective. She took a deep breath instead and said, "You suspended art class."

He tilted his head, confused by this. "Why does *that* bother you?"

"It's my favorite class—the only one I really like."

"It is? I never knew that."

Molly looked over at him and noticed his face had softened. It was true—he really didn't know how much she loved art class.

Because she had never told him.

"I guess I can't expect you to read my mind. I don't exactly do that *sharing feelings* thing very well." And then like a landslide she couldn't control, the words tumbled out of her mouth. "I'm sorry, Dad."

He scooted closer and wrapped his arm around her. "Aww, Turkey. I'm sorry, too—truly."

This filled her with warmth. Turkey was the name he'd always called her when she was little. And she loved it. But it had been years since he'd used it.

And here he was using her favorite childhood name, feeding her pizza, and apologizing. All while wearing those ladybug slippers.

She threw her arms around his neck. "Let's have pizza together more often, Dad."

He squeezed her tightly, then sat back, looking at her wet eyes. This made him ache. "I wish there was some way to fix this. I don't want you to lose art class."

She shrugged. "Well, we could have fixed this a long time ago. I told Trevor how to get out of the makeover, but he didn't want to do it."

Decker's eyes grew big. "You mean, you know how to fix this?"

"Sure. But no one came to ask me. Except I stopped talking to Trevor, so it's not like I gave him much of a chance."

"You're not talking to each other? I thought you two were friends."

"We *were* friends. *Are* friends. I don't know. It's all so hard for me. I made one friend, but now I don't know how to keep him as a friend. No one told me how—it's like I need a rule book or something."

He smiled. "Okay, then. Let's make our own. A friendship rule book." Decker walked across the room and pulled out a pen and paper from the drawer. "I think I know what your first rule should be."

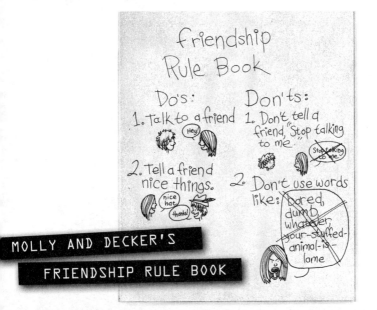

MOLLY AND DECKER'S
FRIENDSHIP RULE BOOK

They laughed, wrote rules, drank soda, and ate pizza from the box. And Molly decided she would put rule number one into effect. She would talk to Trevor. Apparently that's what friends do.

She would tell him she had an idea on how to get rid of Kip Lee. It wasn't foolproof, and there were holes in her plan, but it was a start.

And as long as they did it by three p.m. the next day, it still wasn't too late.

WESTSIDE
MIDDLE SCHOOL

MAKEOVER
FINAL DAY

Libby Gardner

At the end of her
driveway,
looking on the
bright side

7:55 a.m.

The good thing is that Kip gets to finish the
remodel. The bad thing is we lose art class. It's
heartbreaking—I get why Trevor is so upset. But
there just isn't any other way around it.

So I'm going to focus on the positive now.
Today's the last day of the makeover. We're doing
a walk-through while Kip's film crew shoots our
reaction. Well . . . MY reaction. It doesn't look
like Trevor wants to have any part of this.

But everyone else is excited about it, and
since we did all those favors and completed their
design requests, Trevor and I are on our way to
becoming insanely popular. I even overheard Brian
Baker say he would pick Trevor first at kickball.
This means we're both going to have AMAZING things
written under our names in the yearbook . . . I'm
sure of it.

CHAPTER TWENTY

LIBBY ARRIVED AT SCHOOL EARLY SO SHE COULD GET TO Kip's trailer and get started on the tour of the final reveal. In an attempt to be camera-ready, she'd even taken the time to curl her hair and pinch her cheeks for extra color. On the show, this was always the time when the camera would zoom in for a close face-shot to show a person's amazed reaction. So healthy-looking rosy cheeks were essential.

Rounding the corner, she saw Jamie Jennison hobbling down the hall. Libby ran up to her. "Are you okay?"

"That volleyball court . . . the sand had rocks in it. *Rocks*, Libby. I can hardly walk!"

Before Libby could even start with her apology, Becca with Braces charged up to her. "Look at this, Libby!" Becca held her palm out. It was purple.

"What happened to you?" Libby asked.

"The lockers they painted? It comes right off when you touch it. And I heard Savannah Maxwell leaned against her locker and now her *entire* backside is purple. She screeched like a cat dropped in ice water!"

Oh, no! This can't be happening, Libby thought. Everything was coming together so well . . . and now THIS?!

Libby spun away, dizzied by this news. And that's when she saw it: a line outside the school nurse's office. At the end of the line was Mandy Weston, who was pressing her temples.

Libby stumbled over to her. "Wh—why is everyone in line for the nurse?"

"Those new lights . . . they keep flickering. And now a bunch of kids have headaches. Everyone else has lower-back pain; those beanbags are missing *a lot* of beans. So we're all waiting for a magic washcloth. If it weren't for that slushee machine, I'd say the makeover was a bad idea. But that double-berry flavor is to die for." Mandy patted Libby on the shoulder. "Don't worry—it's okay."

Libby's heart pumped double time. "No, this is not okay. No one should be in the nurse's office, no matter how great that slushee machine is. Kip owes me an explanation for all of this!"

She stomped down the hall, flew out the back door, and started to march right up to Kip's trailer.

But he was already outside, pacing the blacktop while he frantically waved his phone in the air. Like he was trying to flag down a rescue plane.

"Two bars! That's all I can get out here? Help a guy out!"

She stepped up next to him, her jaw clenched. Not sure where to start about all the complaints that had just been tossed her way, she said in a sharp tone, "Just use the phone in the office."

Kip gave her a confused look, as if the words *use the phone in the office* were a foreign language.

She folded her arms. "It has push buttons . . . connects into a wall . . . ring a bell?"

He held his hand up. "I'll keep pacing until I get more bars." Kip started to walk away but then glanced back. "Did you need me for something?"

This was it. Her moment. "Could you explain to me why there are rocks in the volleyball sand? And why the locker paint rubs off? And why the majority of the school is in line for the nurse because of headaches and lower-back pain?!"

He studied her with the same confused look he'd had

when she'd spoken of a phone that was connected to a wall. "I . . . I don't know what you're talking about. The slushee machine works perfectly, right?" He winced.

And then it hit her. When he said the slushee machine keeps people from complaining, he meant about his shoddy design materials. This wasn't the first time this had happened!

"You knew the materials were cheap, didn't you? That's why you always bring the slushee machine . . . so we won't complain. But frozen treats or not . . . I'M COMPLAINING!"

He shrugged. "Look, I just do whatever the producers tell me to do. It's not like I'm some *master designer*." And then he laughed.

Libby, however, did not see any humor in this. "I don't see what's funny about this. Most of Westside is waiting in line for magic washcloths. You owe me an explanation."

Kip took a breath and stopped laughing. "Here's the deal. We buy in bulk—it's cheaper that way. There's no way we could afford to install high-end materials. We simply don't get enough advertising revenue." He sighed and continued. "The show is scripted. I just say the words they write for me."

She couldn't believe what she was hearing. On the show, he seemed to know everything about design. She realized then that her second-place idol wasn't who she thought he was—not at all. She leaned in and narrowed her eyes. "You don't even have any training in design, do you?"

"Nope. I was working at Home Depot—the nuts-and-bolts department. I got into design just by watching TV shows. Then I won a reality-show contest by beating out other contestants. The viewers voted for me to get my own show." He glared down at her and smirked. "Libby, all you need is personality and great hair, not talent."

She clutched her heart to keep it from beating out of her chest. This guy, Kip Lee—her second-place IDOL—wasn't a real designer at all.

He was a fraud.

She'd spent so much personal time over the years studying his show. Collecting facts, pictures, and more pictures. She had no idea all those newly made-over schools fell apart the moment the cameras were gone. What a waste!

Oh, no, Libby thought. Wilson's Supply Containment Unit—it was going to be demolished!

She stuck her hands on her hips. Her confident-yet-simultaneously-disgusted stance. "Are you saying you're going to demolish Wilson's Supply Containment Unit and you aren't even a trained designer? And those new shelves are going to fall apart as soon as your trucks pull away?!"

"That's why I've been trying to get better cell phone reception. I've been calling my producer daily to find out what to do. Plus, there's a good chance those shelves could hold up. As long as he doesn't put anything heavy on them. Or light stuff, either, actually." Kip's phone rang, and he quickly looked to see who was calling. "That's my producer. I have to take this call." He turned away from her.

Libby marched back across the blacktop and headed toward the school in search of help.

Winning this contest was the worst thing she could have done as class president. She caused the school to lose art class for *this*? And now Wilson was going to have his closet demolished by someone whose only talent was taking orders from a producer on his cell phone with bad reception. She wished she had just done what was *really* needed for the school—raise money for new art supplies.

But now it was too late.

Marty Nelson

Looking unusually
nervous

10:26 a.m.

I haven't talked to Trevor in a couple of days.
He's been busy helping Mr. Hollywood with this
remodel.

But I have to find Trevor and talk to him about
those rugs for the boys' locker room. See, I got
my info on the dangers of slick floors from an
article in *Junior Survivor* magazine, but I only
skimmed the first couple of paragraphs. Apparently you have to read the ENTIRE article before
you get enough facts to go and ask someone a big
favor.

Fine, lesson learned. But now I've got to find
Trevor, quick!

CHAPTER TWENTY-ONE

O<small>N HIS WAY TO CLASS</small> M<small>ARTY SPOTTED</small> T<small>REVOR AT HIS</small> locker with shoulders so slumped he knew something had to be wrong.

"Spill it." He patted Trevor on the back, but hard enough to knock the breath out of him.

Trevor took a moment to catch his breath, then coughed out, "I have some bad news."

"I have news, too," Marty said.

But Trevor wanted to go first and get this off his chest. There was only so long he could go with shoulders this slumped before he ended up in a chiropractor's office. "The school board got rid of art class this year," he blurted. "They had to pay for the remodel expenses—or hotel and restaurant and designer T-shirt expenses actually. So I quit Libby's design team."

"Whoa. No Art? So rude, man."

"Yeah, but it also means I'm not going to be able to help you get those rugs you wanted." He winced a little. "I understand if you're mad."

"Naw, man. Turns out, I should have read the *entire* article on the dangers of wet tile. Apparently rugs in a bathroom where people are showering can get wet and moldy. Mold spores are in the top fifty leading causes of headaches. I read that in a different article I skimmed. So we can't risk it. Let's leave it how it was."

Trevor let out a sigh of relief. "Honestly, I wish *everything* could go back to how it was," he said.

Marty nodded. "Like I said before, some changes are good. Like moving *Extreme Catfish Hoarders* to Friday nights at eight p.m.? Brilliant. But not all changes are good, and this remodel is one of them."

As they neared their next class, Vice Principal Decker came on over the intercom. "As a reminder, today is the last day of the school remodel. We're almost there! And to celebrate, I'm told today's lunch will be . . . chicken nuggets. Have a good day, Westside." There was the sound of papers crumpling and Decker—though his voice was fainter—kept talking. "I'm sure glad I *brought* my lunch today."

Trevor and Marty looked at each other and covered their mouths, trying to hold back laughs. Did Decker not realize the intercom was still on?

"And I can't believe I agreed to cancel art class just to pay for the expenses of this ridiculous makeover. Oh! Mrs. Baxter, do you have any more pictures of that lovely dog of yours?"

The intercom then clicked off. Trevor and Marty couldn't keep their laughs in any longer. They wondered who would break the news to Decker that the intercom had been on the whole time.

But Trevor stopped laughing when he saw Molly in the distance. She didn't notice him because she was too busy digging for something in her backpack. She looked determined, and Trevor figured there must be something important in there.

Something important . . .

And that's when it hit him. Decker's announcement, Molly's backpack . . . He'd figured out a way to get everything back to how it was!

He grabbed Marty by the arm. "I have it—a way to save art class *and* get Kip Lee out of our school for good!"

Marty rubbed his hands together. He always loved a good plan. "Unload it."

"I'll need your help. The plan involves the school intercom, Molly, Corey, and one big trick."

Marty raised a brow. "You had me at intercom."

Despite her worries that he wouldn't accept her apology, Molly boldly approached Trevor with a prepared apology speech. She had even memorized it and didn't need the note card. Practicing the speech over and over the previous night in front of Miss Frankie, her worn teddy bear from childhood, had really paid off.

As long as Trevor didn't interrupt and stayed completely silent like Miss Frankie, she'd make it through this speech, no problem.

She noticed Trevor was standing outside class talking to Marty. This was not ideal, since Marty was not in the picture when she'd given her practice speech. But she figured she would give Marty that I-need-to-talk look and he'd get the hint.

She approached them while simultaneously giving The Look to Marty. "Trevor, I need to talk to you."

Trevor smiled—the timing of this couldn't be better. "You're just the person we needed to talk to."

"We?" She kept up The Look, but Marty didn't seem fazed.

My soul bear

"Marty and I have a favor to ask."

This wasn't going the way it had gone with Miss Frankie at all. She folded her arms. "But how am I supposed to apologize to you with *him* here?"

"Apologize?" Trevor's voice cracked a little, and he could feel his face turn red.

"Yeah. For not talking to you. I broke my first rule. I have a friendship rule book now, thanks to my dad. But Marty's here, so forget it and just tell me what the favor is," she said.

Trevor wished Marty could disappear because he sure would like to hear more about this apology and what exactly a friendship rule book was. But she looked ready to move on. "I figured out a way to save Art and get rid of Kip Lee at the same time. And I need your help."

Molly narrowed her eyes, unsure if he had thought this through. "What about Libby? Won't she be mad?"

He shrugged. "She didn't seem to get that some things are more important, like art class."

"So are you gonna help us?" Marty asked.

"Save Art? Are you crazy? Of course I will." Molly even smiled a little. "Whatever crazy thing you have planned, I'm in."

Trevor motioned for them to come closer. "Okay, here's the deal. We need your petition, Molly. The one you brought to me earlier where you said all we needed was a majority of student signatures in order to stop the remodel."

She patted her backpack. "Still got it."

"Good. It's not too late—if we get the signatures, we can end this makeover and get Art back."

"You're trying to stop the makeover?" A voice suddenly came from over Molly's shoulder.

Trevor looked up to see Libby standing there. She had heard everything. Oh, no. This was going to upset her to no end.

But Libby squeezed her way into the circle, not looking upset at all. In fact, she was grinning ear to ear. "I'm in, too," Libby said. "Let's go get some signatures."

Vice Principal Decker

Outside his office,
looking pretty proud
of himself

11:17 a.m.

The intercom was on. Yes, I know.

I'd told Kip Lee that I wouldn't announce to the kids that his makeover was the reason art class was suspended. To clarify: I told him I wouldn't PURPOSELY announce it. We never said anything about ACCIDENTAL announcements.

It was all Molly's idea. My daughter is quite the resourceful young lady. I'm glad I know this now—it was about time.

Molly Decker

Making sure she's
out of earshot from
Trevor, Marty, and
Libby

11:18 a.m.

Everything is falling into place: Dad making that
"accidental" announcement. Trevor wanting signatures for the petition.

Everything except for one crucial part. And I
have no idea how we're going to get around this
one. But we have to deal with this—NOW.

CHAPTER TWENTY-TWO

"**H**OLD UP. THERE'S ONE BIG PROBLEM.**" MOLLY** pulled the gang over to a quiet spot by the bathroom. "Trevor and I are the only ones who love art class more than beanbags. How are we ever going to convince enough people to sign the petition? They don't care about Art; they love that slushee machine."

She had a point. But Trevor had the answer. "Ah, see. That's where our pal Corey Long comes in. I saw him getting drawing tips from Mr. Jeffries. He likes Art as much as we do!"

"So? How does that help us?"

Trevor raised a brow. "Remember the hair flip?"

Molly and Libby looked at each other and smiled. How could they forget? At the beginning of the school year,

Corey showed up with a haircut that was short in the back and long in the front. He'd kept it out of his eyes with his signature hair-flip move. It was smooth, suave, and took gobs of talent.

Girls swooned.

Guys imitated.

Corey's hair flip became a sensation. Droves of guys at the school were trying to grow their hair out long on top and flipping it just like Corey. It seemed as though whatever Corey Long thought was cool, others did, too.

Even when they didn't look as cool doing it. Not at all.

"I see what you're getting at." Libby tapped at her chin. "If Corey tells people that art class is cool, then getting the signatures by the end of the day will be a cinch."

Molly narrowed her eyes. "But how in the world will we get him to tell that to everyone?"

Before Trevor could answer, Marty stepped up and answered in his calming eighth grade voice. "Ladies, ladies. I may not be the head writer of a trendy detective show, but I think I've got this all figured out. Trevor said the plan involved the school intercom, so my guess is we'll have Decker add it to his announcements, maybe right after the Pledge of Allegiance."

"Uh . . . pretty close," Trevor said, wondering how to nicely tell him he wasn't actually pretty close. "The plan involves an 'accidental' announcement, just like Decker's—that's where I got the idea."

Molly folded her arms, pleased her idea had inspired his plan.

"We're going to trick Corey by telling him there are some renovations Kip wants him to do in the office," Trevor explained. "I'll start asking him questions about Art, and when I give you the signal, Marty, you'll flip on the intercom. The whole school will hear him talking about how cool Art is."

"And then Libby and I will get signatures," Molly added. "And we'll all meet up by my dad's office at the end of the day."

The four of them put their hands together and yelled their fighting chant.

FOUND IN TREVOR'S NOTEBOOK

Which they then decided was the worst fighting chant ever and vowed to never repeat again.

CHAPTER TWENTY-THREE

LATER THAT DAY, MARTY AND TREVOR JOINED UP NEAR the eighth graders' lockers to find Corey. It wasn't hard to spot him.

The leaning on a locker. The reeking of coolness. The adjusting a few select hairs. Several guys were crowding him, also adjusting select hairs. Without much success.

Hanging back so they could survey the scene, Trevor and Marty watched and waited. "Okay, go tell him that Kip needs him in the office," Marty said.

Trevor hesitated, feeling paralyzed. "Me? I can't talk to him face-to-face. He'll pummel me or trip me—it's an automatic response with him. You should do it."

"But it wouldn't make sense. Why would Kip send *me* to tell him? He'd be suspicious." Marty nudged Trevor in

Corey's direction. "Just keep your feet away from his. It's simple. I'll meet you in the office."

When he said it like that, Trevor had to agree it *did* seem simple. And yet, when it came to Corey, things always resulted in him losing a good portion of his dignity.

"And give me some sort of signal when you want me to turn on the intercom," Marty said as he walked away.

Trevor took a deep breath and tried to convince himself he could do this.

Get in, get out, he coached himself. Don't be intimidated, don't say stupid things, and keep your feet away from his.

Pushing back his shoulders, Trevor took a deep breath to fill his lungs with air and his head with confidence.

It was working.

He strode up to Corey assertively and tapped him on the shoulder. "Kip has some work for us to do in the office. He needs us to go up there."

Corey rolled his eyes. "Now?"

"Yep, now. Follow me." Trevor couldn't believe his self-coaching had worked. He'd said what he needed to say, and now that Corey was going to the office with him, he could move on to the next part of the plan.

"I'm not going with you."

Or not.

Corey knew how to make *everything* difficult. "Why won't you go?"

Corey stepped away from the guys imitating his hair-adjusting and motioned for Trevor to follow him over to his locker. "Look, I never wanted to do this in the first place. My mom forced me because she thought it would help me land an acting audition. I only agreed to do it because of . . ." His voice faded away as if he didn't want to finish his thought.

Trevor leaned in, his eyes big and questioning. "Because of . . . ?"

Corey's face grew a tint redder. "I just feel bad for hurting Libby's feelings at the dance last fall. I'm only doing this for her—so she'll stop being mad at me."

Whoa.

Also: WHOA.

Judging from the fact that Corey was now *seriously* blushing, Trevor realized this wasn't just about getting Libby to stop being mad at him. It was because he liked her.

And since Trevor was Libby's best friend, this moment was now hugely weird.

Corey smirked and looked down at Trevor. "So will Libby be there, too?"

Bingo! This was how he could get Corey up to the office. "Uh . . . sure. Libby will be there," he lied, hoping he could consider it more of an exaggeration. Guilty was not his favorite state of being.

Corey slammed his locker door shut. "Then let's go." He whirled around, and as he and Trevor both stepped forward, the inevitable happened. Feet collided. And Trevor had to admit that all the self-coaching in the world couldn't seem to stop him from tripping on a regular basis.

Unintentional tripping. Really?
Can't I ever catch a break?

FOUND IN TREVOR'S NOTEBOOK

"Dude, I didn't trip you on purpose!" Corey pulled him up off the floor and led the way toward the office.

Trevor struggled to catch up—his ankle hurt from the fall. "Ow." *Step.* "Ow." *Step.* "Ow."

Corey sighed, then stopped in the middle of the hall. "I can*not* believe I'm saying this, but put your hand on my shoulder and I'll help you walk."

"Really? But people will see you being . . . helpful."

"I'm a helpful guy. That's not shocking."

"But to *me*."

"True, that's shocking. People will talk."

And then Trevor couldn't believe what Corey said next.

"But whatever. Who cares?"

At that moment, Trevor honestly didn't know if they were enemies or friends. But his ankle was throbbing, so he put his hand on Corey's shoulder anyway. "Thanks for the help."

The two made their way down the hall, through crowds of students and amid giggles and whispers.

"Just ignore them," Corey instructed. "And always keep your head up."

Trevor took his advice and lifted his chin. And when he did, he noticed that he was making eye contact with

people as they passed by. Soon, all the giggles and whispers stopped.

"That really works!" Trevor yelped.

"Years of practice. I can teach you a lot."

Wow, Trevor thought. Corey Long—King of the Jerks,
Master of Meanness, Emperor of Non-Empathy—is being
NICE to me. And instead of ruining my reputation, he's
teaching me how to save it. This day is officially bizarre.

Dear The Congress,
    It is hereby noted that on
this day, the fourteenth of
March, Corey (middle name
unknown) Long went out of
his way to help me instead of
hurting me. So therefore,
forthright, and/or hither. (I'm
not sure if I am using these
words correctly, but I'm sure
you require them.)

    Therefore, I request that
this day shall now be a
national holiday, where
schools and banks and
libraries are closed to honor
this great act. But please
don't close Burger King or
Video Palace.

    Considerately and seventh gradely yours,
        Trevor Jones

They neared the office, and Trevor could see Marty inside waiting for him. As he leaned on Corey's shoulder, he remembered what he was there to do: trick Corey into talking on the intercom. But he simply couldn't—there was no way he could go through with it. Not now. Corey was finally being borderline friendly to him.

He had to find a way out of this mess, quick.

Trevor Jones

Outside the office,
a little limpy

12:44 p.m.

I tried telling him my ankle had gotten worse and I needed to go to the nurse. But he reminded me that we'd have to go through the office to get to her station anyway.

So that didn't work.

So then I started coughing, begging to go get a drink of water. Which I did, but that only took a whopping thirteen seconds, and we were right back where we started: me with a swollen ankle, a nurse's station by the office, and Corey suddenly wanting to be a helpful person. Not a good combination when you have a plan that needs to be implemented. And a gang of helpers expecting it to work.

I guess I need to go to Plan C: fake a bee attack.

CHAPTER TWENTY-FOUR

BEFORE TREVOR COULD FAKE AN ONCOMING BEE SWARM, Corey pushed through the door to the front office. "Let's go get you some ice for that ankle," he said.

Marty was sitting in the secretary's chair, flipping through pictures of her beagle. "I know I have more around here somewhere," the secretary said as she searched through her drawers. Then she popped up tall. "The storage closet! That's where I have those pictures of Bugsy in his Halloween costume! I dressed him as an ear of corn. So cute I would've eaten him, except . . . I'd never do that."

The secretary looked up and noticed that Trevor and Corey had entered the room. She narrowed her eyes. "Did Decker call you boys in? Are you in trouble?"

Trevor wasn't sure how to respond. *Stall* was the only

solution he could come up with. "Us? We . . . uh . . ."

She narrowed her eyes even more.

"Kip asked us to help with some renovations in here," Corey said calmly. "Also, I need to get some ice for Trevor's ankle. And I'd sure like to see those Halloween pictures of Bugsy."

The secretary flashed a big smile. "You're so helpful, Corey. What would we do without you around here?"

Trevor remembered that Corey had a way of snowing teachers and faculty. Also: girls. Also: everyone else.

"Be right back with those pictures," she said as she disappeared into the supply closet.

Corey looked over at Marty. "What are *you* doing in here?"

"I help the secretary out during my elective class. Oh, hey! Speaking of electives . . ."

Trevor took a step back out of Corey's sight and made an X sign with his hands, signaling for him to stop the plan and *not* turn on the intercom.

Corey leaned over the desk and tapped on it to get Marty's attention. "What did you want to say about electives? You kinda spaced out there, man."

Marty *had* spaced out, because he was dealing with lots of information all at once. Questions, dog photos, and a signal from Trevor. A signal! He must want him to turn on the intercom.

"Trevor was wondering what elective he should take next time," Marty said as he slyly leaned back and clicked the ON button for the intercom.

"Me? No, no, I wasn't wondering that." Trevor vigorously waved his hands, trying to get Marty to turn it off. But no such luck.

Corey was already scratching his chin, deep in thought. "Favorite elective? That's easy." Corey's voice was upbeat—almost enthusiastic—and he spoke with enough volume to be picked up by the intercom.

The *all-school* intercom.

"Most people don't know this, but my favorite class is Art. Mr. Jeffries, man . . . that dude is the coolest. He's been teaching me how to draw, and hopefully I'll publish my own comic. You know, be in newspapers and stuff—on the Internet."

Trevor swallowed hard. *Wow, this is going further than I imagined. He's admitting everything! Even future job prospects! I'm doomed.*

Corey turned to Trevor. "Do you think Libby would like it if I drew her something?"

Oh, no. He's bringing up Libby!

"Maybe you shouldn't talk about . . ." Trevor kept making big eyes and bizarre hand signals to Marty, hoping he'd cut it off. But instead Marty leaned back and turned up the volume.

Which was when it all went from bad to catastrophic.

"I kind of, sort of, pretty much . . . like her." Corey blushed. "What do you think, bro? Does she like me?"

The only redeeming thing that Trevor could find about this moment was that Corey wasn't using Libby's first *and* last name over the all-school intercom. There were two other Libbys at Westside. Libby Shulman, eighth grader and the daughter of the librarian. And Libby Carter, seventh grader, who played third base on the softball team and wore striped tube socks, even with a skirt. Could be *either one*.

"You guys need to help me," Corey continued. "You gotta get Libby Gardner to like me!"

I'm dead.

"I found those pictures!" The secretary had suddenly returned.

Marty jumped up and flicked off the intercom. Trevor had to quickly find a way to get them out of there.

"I guess I was wrong about Kip needing our help. He's not here." Trevor stared at the exit sign. "I'm gonna go get ice for my ankle. See you later."

Trevor limped toward the nurse's office and glanced back to see Corey exiting through the office door with a *very* confused look on his face. And his face was something Trevor needed to stay far, far away from. He hoped his ankle looked bad enough that Nurse Quincy would feel it necessary to keep him there and put a washcloth on his forehead for the *rest of his life*.

Trevor Jones

Outside the nurse's
office, with a pass
back to class

12:50 p.m.

Nurse Quincy kept me in there for ten minutes. TEN
MINUTES! I tried to convince her that my ankle was
more than likely broken, maybe in multiple places,
like the knee.

But she poked and prodded and said I only had
a bruise.

I explained to her that a bruise is technically a RUPTURE OF CAPILLARIES AND LEAKAGE OF RED
BLOOD CELLS, so how could she possibly expect me
to attend class? Ever again?!

She said I'd be fine.

I didn't tell her that if I ran into Corey
Long my injuries would be MUCH worse. Maybe even
too much for her magic washcloth to handle. The
fact that I got Corey to admit he likes Libby is
one thing. But getting the guy to say it OVER
THE INTERCOM is one of those things that should
require a lifetime visit to the nurse's office.

But no, she wouldn't even take the time to cover my forehead with a washcloth.

So here I go . . . back out into the world. Knowing that more than likely I will end up with Corey's fist landing somewhere on my face. Or stomach. Or soul.

I'm sure he's capable of that.

[gazes off in deep thought for a moment, then rubs hands together]

But not if I can avoid him.

CHAPTER TWENTY-FIVE

FOR THE REST OF THE DAY, TREVOR DID WHATEVER IT took to stay out of Corey's way. He avoided him in the halls by pushing his back up against the lockers when he passed. But, strangely, he ended up with a purple backside.

He then hid in the library, but felt a slight headache come on from the flickering lights.

Finally, he attempted to stay out of Corey's way by hiding out behind the meditation fountain, but the water was leaking and he ended up with soggy tennis shoes.

What is going on?! he wondered.

In order to stay dry, paint-less, and headache-free, he decided he wouldn't stop at his locker and just go directly from class to class. To accomplish this, he threw all his books in his backpack and lugged it around so he wouldn't be vulnerable by his locker. Though his backpack was now as heavy as a fourth grader, it had to be done.

He had to be unnoticeable. Practically invisible.

Trevor Jones was in stealth mode.

Or so he thought.

As he sat in language arts class (first one there!), Trevor wondered if Molly and Libby had been able to get any signatures yet. But more importantly, he wondered if Libby had heard what Corey admitted over the intercom. What was her reaction? Did she like him back? *Should* she? Corey was kind of a jerk, but then sometimes . . . he wasn't.

The students started to fill in the classroom, and Libby quietly slid into the seat next to him. Immediately, Trevor could tell she'd heard Corey's announcement. It was her cheeks. Lobster red.

Libby, normal

Libby, after Accidental Announcement from Corey (not normal, right?)

FOUND IN TREVOR'S NOTEBOOK

Libby was silent, but he knew he needed to get her talking. Otherwise, she'd start the hair-chew-twirl thing, and soon she'd look like a Muppet. There were a few minutes before class started, so it was time for a heart-to-heart.

He leaned over to her. "Obviously you heard the announcement."

"Yep." She still looked straight ahead. Still with lobster cheeks.

"Do you want to talk about—"

"Nope."

"Are you okay—"

"Don't know."

"Can you—"

"Not sure."

It was obvious to him that she wasn't ready to share yet. Timing was critical in getting info out of Libby. He needed to change the subject.

"So I have one question—"

"No."

"Libby, seriously. I won't even mention Corey."

She turned to him, the color on her cheeks settling back into normal territory. More like fruit-punch-colored. "Promise you won't mention him?"

"Promise."

She calmly folded her hands. "Ask it."

"Did you get any signatures yet?"

She laughed. "Any?" Libby pointed over to the other side of the room. "Check out Molly."

Gliding up and down the aisles was Molly, quickly getting signatures with hardly any effort. "Sign here to get art class back. Thank you. Sign here. Thank you." She looked up at him and winked.

The plan was working.

"When he-who-shall-not-be-mentioned got on the intercom and said Art is cool, *everyone* wanted to take the class," Libby explained. "Plus, it wasn't just a few people who were upset with the makeover. Just about everyone is. Apparently those beanbags really hurt your lower back— no lumbar support at all. And they don't even care about the slushee machine anymore—it's leaking everywhere. So this is all a win-win!"

"That's awesome." Trevor was excited to hear the news and also excited that Libby was getting back to her regular self: nice coloring, chatty demeanor.

"So about Corey's announcement . . . the part about you . . ."

She quickly turned back to face the front. "Not now."

"But do you—"

"Stop."

"Can't you—"

"Shh. Or I'm telling your mom."

And that was that. No more discussion on Libby's thoughts about Corey. But truthfully—for some strange reason—he suddenly realized he really *didn't* want to know how she felt about Corey.

Not one bit.

Trevor Jones

Looking rather
confused

2:55 p.m.

Fine, I want to know a LITTLE bit. But then again,
it's not any of my business. But then again, what
if she likes him and doesn't know what a jerk he
is? But then again, what if she DOESN'T like him
and doesn't know that sometimes he isn't a jerk at
all? This is so confusing.

   [sighs deeply]

   I need a nap.

CHAPTER TWENTY-SIX

LIBBY AND **M**OLLY HAD WORKED TOGETHER TO COLLECT signatures throughout the day. They had met between classes and passed the petition back and forth without even having to use words or explanations. Just a wink and a knowing nod.

It was as if this common goal had given them a new way to communicate with each other. Libby couldn't help but categorize it as "almost friendly."

It was totally weird.

But she liked it.

A few minutes before school let out, both the girls got hall passes and rushed over to meet at Libby's locker. "Got enough?" Libby asked.

Molly smiled. "Yep. Let's do this."

Luckily, Molly knew the shortest route to Vice Principal Decker's office: cut through the library, walk briskly through the teachers' lounge (but act like you're supposed to be in there!), then turn right out the back exit and head down the hall behind Decker's office.

Libby power walked, as usual, and was surprised to find Molly could keep up with her. This was the first friend (or person suddenly acting friend-like) who ever walked with her, stride for stride.

Pretty cool.

They hustled through the library and sped through the teachers' workroom. Luckily, they maintained a look of "I'm allowed to be in here," so no teachers asked questions. They were in the clear.

Almost.

When they turned the corner to head down the back hall, *wham!* They ran straight into a pair of size twelve Italian leather sandals.

Kip Lee glared down at the papers in Libby's hands. "A petition?" Before Libby could answer, he reached out and snatched the papers away from her. "No way. I'm on deadline! We need this to air next week—we can't afford to air a rerun because of another one of these petitions. Our ratings!"

Molly stepped up closer and narrowed her eyes at Kip. She wasn't about to let him talk to Libby like that. "Listen up. We don't care about your ratings—"

But Libby put her hand on Molly's arm, stopping her. As much as she appreciated her help—this super awesome friend-like behavior—there were some things Libby felt *she* needed to say to Kip. She gave Molly a knowing nod that said: *I got this.*

Pushing her shoulders back, Libby gathered her nerve and locked eyes with Kip. "There's a rule in design, Mr. Lee. And yes, I learned it on a TV show, but it wasn't yours. And here's the rule: always listen to your client. Trevor mentioned needing better pencil sharpeners. I suggested higher-wattage lightbulbs. Marty wanted rugs. Savannah wanted mirrors. But what did we get? Headaches and lower-back pain and lunches that can't be eaten without spilling them into our shoes."

Kip flinched. "I told you—the materials are cheaper when we buy in bulk. It's just the way it's done!"

Libby threw her hands in the air. "That's not the change I wanted for our school. We deserve better—a place that's unique, comfortable, and without beanbags that swallow you whole. And more importantly, we deserve an art class with all the supplies we need."

Before Kip could respond, Vice Principal Decker stepped out of his office. He looked at the papers in Kip's hand and said, "Aha! That expense report. I need to turn this in to the school board today." He took the papers from Kip and looked them over.

Molly and Libby locked eyes and didn't say a word. They didn't have to—they'd done it. The petition was in Decker's hands.

Decker peeked at the girls over the paper. "A petition? After all this, you want to kick the TV show out?"

Libby started to respond, but Molly leaned into her and whispered, "I can handle this." After all, this was *her* dad.

"The students don't want a makeover, Dad. They want Art. And according to the fine print, if we get signatures from a majority of students, the makeover can be stopped and they can't air the show."

Decker took a deep breath and dropped his shoulders. "Mr. Lee, I'm sorry to have to do this, but the students have spoken. I'll have to ask you to stop production and leave the premises. Immediately."

It took everything in them for Libby and Molly not to squeal with delight.

And it took everything Decker had to not crack a smile.

Vice Principal Decker

Totally cracking a smile

3:05 p.m.

Molly and I planned all that. She told me she'd steer Libby through the teachers' workroom and down the back hallway next to my office door.

We planned that I would snatch the petition from Kip if he intercepted it. And we planned for my reaction to be as authentic as possible.

It was the fine print. We checked it again and read that the administration can't have ANY influence on the signing of a petition—it has to be all student led. So I couldn't let Kip know I knew about it.

Yes, that means I am being slightly tricky. But life often presents you with difficult decisions. You have to weigh the consequences.

Molly Decker

Shocked and amazed

3:06 p.m.

Whoa. Seriously . . . whoa. I had NO IDEA Libby had that in her. I mean, I've given people a "talking—to" before, but Libby gave that man a SCHOOLING.

I never thought I'd say this, but I think I can learn a lot from that girl.

And Dad?

[scuffs boots on the floor]

He did pretty good. Actually, REALLY good. He may even deserve a new pair of ladybug slippers.

CHAPTER TWENTY-SEVEN

KIP HEADED DOWN THE HALL BUT TURNED BACK TO ADD one more thing. "One more thing!" He wagged a finger at them. "The small print on the Web site says the expenses are not refundable. You still owe us the money—there's no way you can trick your way out of that one." He smirked. "And I need it today . . . before we leave."

He turned and sauntered off as if he didn't have a care in the world. Like he'd said that line many times before.

They all stood in silence as they watched Kip disappear around the corner—just as Trevor turned around the same corner.

"Well, I don't see any other choice, kids." Decker's voice was soft. "I'll have to go to the board and get Kip a check—quickly."

Trevor planted his feet firmly. "There has to be another way. I don't want to keep any of this new stuff—I just want an art teacher."

Libby bit at her lip. "But we don't even have time to go home and cook stuff for a bake sale."

They all glared at Decker, hoping a brilliant plan would hatch from his balding head.

"I have a plan—a pretty brilliant one."

But Decker wasn't the one who said it; the voice came from behind. They all whirled around and saw Cindy Applegate peeking around the corner. She was holding a poster board and her favorite pink gel pen.

"It won't be a bake sale . . . it'll be a *school* sale," Cindy said with all the charm she could pull together (everyone was looking at her, after all). "I do have amazing poster-making skills—skills that Kip did not value—so I am willing to help you all out. If you don't mind the poster being in pink. That's really the only option I'm giving: pink or nothing."

Molly folded her arms tightly and squinted at her. "What are you talking about?"

Cindy marched up to them and waggled her poster board around. "We can sell all the furniture and accessories that Kip brought. We'll set it all out on the school lawn, and people can buy items as they go through the car-pool line. I will stand at the entrance with my charming poster and BAM! We'll make all the money back!"

"But school is out in a few minutes," Libby said. "How will we have time?"

Cindy shrugged. "I dunno. I like *saying* things, not *doing* them."

Marty then stepped into the middle of the group. "The intercom! Decker can announce we need all hands on deck to pull out all this furniture to the lawn. I will stand outside and organize everyone."

Trevor nodded. "This could work."

Libby smiled at him. "It really could."

Decker raised a finger in the air, and with a smile on his face he said, "To the intercom!"

With the help of every single student, they managed to get all the items outside in time for the car pool. And Cindy even had enough time to make all the posters they needed—supercute and everything.

By the time the last few cars were coming through the car-pool line, Libby had managed to add up all their money. She was all smiles until she got to the very last dollar. "Oh, no! We're short fifty-two dollars!"

They looked around the yard, but it was empty. They had sold every last piece. "What could we possibly sell?"

"Need help, Libby?" Corey Long had walked up beside her.

"Yes! We ran out of things to sell. We need something awesome . . . and quick!"

He took a deep breath because he really didn't know if she would think this was awesome or not. Corey reached into his backpack and pulled out his comic book, all complete. "Want to sell this?"

She flipped through it, and her eyes lit up. "You drew this, Corey?"

He kicked at some nonexistent dirt. "Yeah, no. You know . . . sure."

"It's awesome! A little over the top in this chapter on cafeteria food, and you need an emotional arc, but overall . . . awesome." She clutched the book and looked up at him, smiling. "You mean you'd really sell it, just so we can keep Mr. Jeffries?"

"Well, yeah." He gripped the back of his neck. All this niceness was making him uncomfortable. Though he wanted to tell her more—that he was doing this for her, not just for Mr. Jeffries . . . except the words wouldn't come. So instead he shrugged and smiled at her.

Libby wasn't sure why Corey was being so nice, but she knew she liked it. "Thanks," she said softly.

Corey blushed, then grabbed the comic book and lifted it in the air. "Anyone want to buy this? Fifty-two dollars! Anyone?!"

"I'll take that." Wilson barged up to him and handed the money over to Libby. "I have to find out what happens."

Libby stuffed all the money in a plastic bag and rushed across the blacktop to Kip's SUV, which was just about to pull away. "Tell your producer we got the money!" She wiggled it in the air.

He looked at the money and then at her. "Impressive, young lady. You might just have a bright future in TV producing."

Libby narrowed her eyes and squared up her shoulders. "TV producing? Wow—that's awesome! I've always thought of that as my backup backup plan. Drive safely!"

She patted his door, then twirled away and skipped off. She didn't even wait for Kip's response, because there was something else on her mind—*one* more task that needed to be done to finish off this makeover.

One of Kip's crew members

Looking around, nervous, also excited

3:05 p.m.

Bro, I can't work for that guy anymore! He's a fraud. Doesn't even know the difference between a hammer and a drill.

I'm going to stay on and work for you guys, if you'll have me. Documenting the middle school species is WAY more interesting.

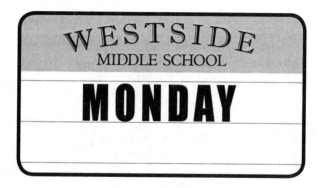

Wilson

Satisfied
(sort of)

8:25 a.m.

I spent my entire weekend here cleaning up the mess and repainting all these lockers back to their original color: squirrel.

But my Supply Containment Unit? Don't want to talk about that, actually.

[paces]

It was torn apart, and Kip never put in those new shelves. So I don't know what to do with it. Like I said . . . I'd rather not talk about it.

But something good did come of this. They left behind one of Kip's items. So I installed it in Mr. Jeffries's room—figured he could use some relaxation after forcing him to pack up and move out. I did check it out to make sure it worked. . . . Quality control is part of my job description.

I'm very good at my job.

CHAPTER TWENTY-EIGHT

LIBBY DIDN'T GO TO HER USUAL LUNCH SPOT. THOUGH she was relieved to see the school get back to normal, there was still one more task that needed to be done.

Wilson's Supply Containment Unit.

It had been partially torn apart, but Kip had never gotten good enough cell reception to find out from the producer how to fix it.

And if there was one thing in the world that Libby Gardner loved most, it was taking on a project. Especially a design project.

She spent her lunch period reorganizing Wilson's closet. It was alphabetized, color coded, and given new lighting. *Good* lighting.

Word spread quickly of the closet makeover, and Wilson was brought over by a group of students for the unveiling—the same way they did on *Trick Out My School.*

Libby looked on proudly. She realized she didn't need Kip's feedback to discover that design—just like a political career—was her calling. Only twelve years old and everything figured out.

Nice.

"Great design, Libby." Suddenly Savannah Maxwell had appeared. She was peering inside Wilson's closet and nodding with approval. "Good use of space. Color. And the lighting, of course. Love. It."

Libby wiggled with excitement. Savannah Maxwell was saying nice things about her design . . . in public! If only she hadn't said those things about her not being a good president in public.

"I was thinking . . ." Savannah said as she flipped her impossibly silky hair over her shoulder. "What if you came over to my house today and helped redesign my bedroom? With your talent, I'm sure you could do wonders. Just throwing it out there . . . Give me your first thought."

Libby looked her over, her eyes landing on her designer boots. *Where DID she get those?*

That was her first thought. But what Libby said out loud was her second thought.

Libby Gardner

Next to Wilson's
newly designed
containment unit—
smirking

3:01 p.m.

I told her NO WAY. I wasn't about to apply my skills to her room. I'd rather save them for something the school needs.

Plus, Trevor had a point—as usual. There WAS a pattern forming. First Jessica Lymon and now Savannah. I need to stop making friends with people who stomp all over my feelings.

I need friends who GET what I'm trying to do. Even if I take the wrong route getting there sometimes. And when I power walk, I need a friend who can keep up with me.

[clasps hands together and smiles]

It just didn't occur to me until now that IT IS NOT Savannah Maxwell.

CHAPTER TWENTY-NINE

"**A**RE YOU READY TO SEE THE AWESOMENESS?" TREVOR gripped the knob on his bedroom door before opening it—he wanted to make the big reveal as dramatic as possible. (For ratings.) (Actually, just Libby's rating.)

She crossed her arms and shot him a smirk. "Ready, Captain."

"What you are about to witness will surprise and amaze you." He gestured like he was introducing a circus act. "I, Trevor Jones, ordinary seventh grader who can't stand change . . . will now reveal my newly rearranged bedroom. Behold!" He flung his door open.

Libby took three steps forward, surveyed the room, and sighed. What she saw was not terribly surprising. In fact, she'd expected this.

"Trevor, all you did was angle your desk diagonally."

"Right?! On the *diagonal*!" He paced his plush-carpeted floor. "Do you have any idea how long it took for me to come up with that brilliant design concept? It's amazing, right? I love it!"

He hated it.

And Libby had known him long enough to realize this.

"May I?" She placed her hands on the front of his desk.

He shrugged. "Sure."

Libby pushed it several inches back, to where it had been originally. "That's what *I* would do if I were designing this room." She stepped back and proudly looked at her work.

Trevor scratched his chin. "Wow, you're right. That's pretty brilliant."

But then she glanced around and noticed one more thing that needed to be moved.

"Since you're so open to change now, we can put this away." She reached for his top shelf and grabbed his one stuffed animal still left out in the open.

It was his old Mickey Mouse toy—ragged and missing an eye and an ear. Not the most handsome little guy. But Trevor thought he was cool, in a ripped and torn sort of way. Molly would probably approve.

Except he had to admit, Libby was very good at design. And also good at making him change his ways for the better. So maybe it was time to embrace change—completely embrace it.

Plus, did he really want to be twenty-five years old with a stuffed animal on his shelf?

Libby tucked Mickey Mouse inside his closet, along with the rest of his toys. "There. Now your room looks perfect for a twelve-year-old boy." She cleared her throat. "*Guy*, actually."

They smiled at each other.

"Thanks, Lib."

"Now, let's get started reorganizing your binder!" Libby said as she skipped off downstairs.

"Be right there."

Before closing the door to his bedroom, he did one last thing.

ROBIN MELLOM used to teach middle schoolers and now she writes about them. (Any resemblance between fictional characters and her previous real-life students are purely coincidental. Probably.)

She is also the author of *The Classroom: The Epic Documentary of a Not-Yet-Epic Kid, The Classroom: Student Council Smackdown!,* and *Ditched: A Love Story.* She lives with her husband and son on the central coast of California.

Visit www.robinmellom.com for exclusive CLASSROOM content!

- Documentary outtakes!
- Inside sneak peeks!
- News on upcoming books!
- Answers to your questions!

(And don't forget to follow Robin on Twitter @robinmellom.)

Through a freak incident involving a school bus, a Labrador retriever, and twenty-four rolls of toilet paper, **STEPHEN GILPIN** knew that someday he would be an artist. He applied himself diligently, and many years later he has found himself the illustrator of around thirty children's books. He lives in Hiawatha, Kansas, with his genius wife, Angie, and a whole bunch of kids. Visit his Web site at www.sgilpin.com.